MICKA

MICKA

FRANCES KAY

PICADOR

First published 2010 by Picador
an imprint of Pan Macmillan, a division of Macmillan Publishers Limited
Pan Macmillan, 20 New Wharf Road, London N1 9RR
Basingstoke and Oxford
Associated companies throughout the world
www.panmacmillan.com

ISBN 978-0-330-51382-1

An extract from this novel, 'The Tale of Micka's Christmas',
was published in *Tyneside Tales* by Endpapers Publishers, 2005.

1 3 5 7 9 8 6 4 2

A CIP catalogue record for this book is available from
the British Library.

Typeset by Ellipsis Books Limited, Glasgow
Printed by CPI Mackays, Chatham ME5 8TD

Visit **www.picador.com** to read more about all our books
and to buy them. You will also find features, author interviews and
news of any author events, and you can sign up for e-newsletters
so that you're always first to hear about our new releases.

for my dear friend Nicci Crowther
who loved stories

CHAPTER 1

1994, December

I had the dream again last night. About the fish that talked.

I was wearing my red jersey. Sitting down by the canal where the wall is broken.

Red is my best colour.

The fish has eyes like a baby, eyelashes and all, two on the one side of its head. Head flat like a pancake. Grey and only a bit shiny, same as a metal bucket. It talks at me in a whisper, like it's breathing in instead of out. Like a voice from the grave. Like one of those things from Kevin's comics you can't kill that looks straight ahead.

I asked Mam could I have a little pup for my birthday and it could sleep on my bed. I would call it Zak.

My birthday came. I was ten, but there was no pup. Everyone was gone when I got up. Mam was away to the SS to ask why no giro came. Kevo my brother stayed out all night. Sometimes my Gran calls round but she had to go to

Peterhead to see her son, that's my Uncle Michael, Mikey, we call him.

There was a letter on the table with my name, Micka, writ on it. Inside was a card with happy birthday yer little toerag. That's Kevo. He writes backways because he's left-handed.

I was hungry but there wasn't anything till Mam went to the shops. There was tea but no milk. So I went down Royts Lane where the trailers are. Good things happen there. I know a boy Bluey, short for Blue Eyes, that's how gypsies call their kids; not names like we have, but how they look. Monkey, Pricky, Dilly and Nan they are called. One is called Cricket. I asked why. Bluey wouldn't say. It is for something dirty the women made up. They don't need our kind of names for where they live and what they do. Blue says never to say gypsies, only travellers. Never to say rats, you say pigs with long tails, and they all know what that is. There is bad luck in some words, and if I said the wrong one I would bring a curse on Bluey or maybe not see him again.

He told me words for wagging off school. He's never in school for more than two weeks because of the travelling. He's been to school in Scotland and all, but he can't read hardly. The words he knows are

on the wag

mitching

sagging

bunking.

I told Bluey about my dream coming again. He said to ask Babs (that's his Nan) what about it. We went to her trailer and the door was broke and swinging open. She never goes inside in the day, even if it's snowing or raining or thunder. She sleeps in there, is all.

Babs was sitting small on an old bread box and in front of her was the fire made of a white door smashed up and she had the old black kettle resting on the wood of the fire to make her tea. Her face is like it has never been washed, real old brown colour, and where the lines are I think she rubs black stuff in. If I would touch that face, it would feel stiff and warm like an old shoe.

I told Babs my dream and she spat in the fire. She pinched her eye at me and I stared back like I wasn't scared. She said, Don't be telling anyone about that dream.

~ Why?

~ Have you ever been hurt bad?

~ No.

~ Have you ever hurt anyone bad?

~ No.

She spit in the fire again and her spit wobbled and hissed on the white wood. Her spit was green.

~ Can't tell you nothing if you lie to me.

~ I'm no liar, Babs.

~ You don't give me my name, you gorgio boy.

3

She stood up and her plate with bread on it turned over and slid down her coat and fell in the ashy mud.

~ Bluey, take him away, he's a no-good chavvy.

We went away. Blue said I wasn't to mind her, she's mad anyway, and the muskras give her gin when she's lelled for choring in the market. I like Bluey's talk but I run behind it.

Blue goes to another trailer with a pen outside. Lying on the ground with not even a blanket, seven pups sucking, and their mother. She growls at me and shows some teeth.

~ Scared to go in, Micka?

~ No.

I climb the walls of the pen and straight off she bites me a good one on the leg. I kick her and she goes flying. Growling and snapping and all the pups tag along behind her, screaming.

~ You want a pup? says Blue. Take one.

I pick one. The maddest of the lot. Black and white with soft droppy ears the shape of pears just. When it tries to walk it gans along crooked, its leg bent wrong.

Blue bangs on the side of the trailer with his fist and a Romany man comes out. Black hair and black eyebrows. Drunk so he has to hold both hands on the side of the trailer to stand still.

~ Ey, Petey, he's taking a pup.

Blue winks at me and folds his arms like a man.

I thought the Romany would hit me but he only did a hop

to the side of the pen and grabbed the gate and stared at me, shaking all over.

~ Dem pups is worth five guineas.

~ I've no money. Bluey said I could have one.

~ Did he so?

He had no teeth in front and his tongue was black like Babs' kettle. He was rolling a fag and his hand shook and the baccy fell out and he ground it in the dirt cursing.

~ Can I have it, then?

He took the pup off me and turned it upside down and poked its belly and lifted up its tail and put his black finger into its mouth, and all the while the pup was still and quiet. Then he pulled on its bad leg, trying to straighten out the crook. Blue nodded at me. Romany man gave me back the pup.

~ Yeah. You can take the jukel.

He cuffed Bluey on the side of his head.

~ And don't you go giving no more away.

First thing when I got home, I had to find a box and put the pup under my side of the bed. In our flats pets are banned. I didn't want anyone to see him till he was trained and all, then maybe he could live outside.

In the kitchen Mam was crying. Sitting at the table with the bags of shopping still full and the tins and the bread packets spilling out on the floor and she was not seeing it.

I went round by the bins and got a good box. The pup

was quiet all the while inside my strip as good as gold. I put him in the box and shoved it under the bed. It fit all right after a bit of shoving.

~ Can I have some milk?

~ What you want milk for?

~ Mam. I'm hungry, give us some.

I went through the bags of the shopping. Bread. Tea. Milk. Biscuits. Sugar. Fags. Mam does not buy much.

~ Want some toast, Mam?

She stopped sniffing then.

~ You're a good boy, Michael. You'll see me right, won't you?

I put the milk in a cup and took it to the pup. He licked it off my fingers. Got sharp teeth. Every time he squealed or bit I tapped him on the nose. Training. This is how he has to learn his manners.

When it was night I took him up in the bed with me. Kevo never came home that night so we stretched out. The pup soft like a rubber baby toy. Smell of Royts Lane on his fur. He licked my face and I felt the velvet of his little face on my mouth.

I went to school again. If it's your birthday you get to tell about it. I wanted to tell about the present that my Mam and my brothers gave me. Zak the pup. And if I wag off too much they will send the cruelty man around again. In school they have hot pipes by the kitchen you can lean your back on.

The pup moaned a lot when I left. I put some clothes in the box with him so he could learn my smell. Maybe when he is trained he could come to school with me. He would like the warm there. He bit the side off the box and I had to tap him a lot on the nose. He is getting trained a lot. There was no milk again so he has to learn about this.

In school after I told about my birthday it was playtime. I was cold going out. Miss Glennie said, Where is your coat, Michael?

~ Forgot it, Miss.

~ You can stay in and help me by sorting the crayons for the infants' class. Just today.

~ Okay, Miss.

The babies' class crayons. The blue wax ones are like water; they melt the easiest on the radiator. The yellow is the hardest; it never melts, only goes into little chips. The red is the best; when it melts, it mixes with all the others and you can make up new colours with it.

Then the new boy came to sort crayons too. He never asked Miss. He is bigger than me.

~ You're doing it wrong, wanker.

~ Fuck off.

~ Fuck off yourself.

7

~ I'll tell Miss.

New boy picked the skin inside my wrist and twisted it between his fingers and his teeth ground like he was eating aniseed balls. I shut my mouth and no noise came out. I kicked his leg on the bone bit where I know it hurts the worst; he looked murder at me but he made no sound. Hard, like. He kicked me back but I could dodge him easy. Miss Glennie saw and made us stand one each end of the table. New boy smiled and shook his head and his hair flopped over his face. He has a bad smile. He is called Lorry. Like a lorry, and his last name is Parker.

After dinner break we wagged off. He says he has a great life. He lives mostly in the park. He's made a den by the pond and he says he catches ducks and cooks them on a fire when it's dark and the keeper's locked the gates. He showed me the black stick he shoves up the ducks to roast them, and the ashes of his fire, and the hole in the fence by the pond where he can squeeze through and catch the ducks with his bare hand. I dared him to show me, catch a duck right then. He said he could but he wasn't hungry right then. I said I was. He said, If you want one so bad, you do it.

I went and squat down by the hole in the fence. The ducks are a dolly kind, smoothy brown heads with white bands around their necks. Where the brown is it looks like the velvet part of the pup's face. I would love to touch that part. Lorry said where the white band is you can squeeze them by the

8

neck dead. He kept saying, Go on, do it. I reached out but then Lorry punched me in the back and shouted there was an old woman coming with her dog.

We said we would wag off school the next day and go and buy chips. He has money. He showed it me. He wants to come to my house but I can't go to his. He made me tell about Bluey and the trailers and Royts Lane and the pup. It's not fair that I have told him everything (except I wouldn't tell him my dream), but he has told me nothing, like about his Mam and Dad and if he has any brothers or what. And when I tell him stuff about Kevo and Lee and the rest he laughs like he has a sore throat. When he laughs he shakes his hair and it flops in his eyes like a girl's hair.

Some friend I've picked.

THE SECRET LOGBOOK OF THE BOY FEARLESS FERELON.

I can call myself any name I want. I choose the name Fearless Ferelon. It is a kind of a hawk and a boy at the same time. That is only one of the amazing ideas in my head that I will put down in this book when I feel like it. I have more fun with ideas than with what I have actually done in my life so far. Ideas are as big as you want, and they do whatever you want, they grow bigger like the beanstalk in the giant story. No one ever stands in the way of your mind. Although of course I am hoping my life will become more interesting as I try more things out.

Even the way I was born was quite interesting. It was in the street. It was a sort of accident, when my mother, who is called Josie, was knocked down by a motorbike while she crossed the road to buy some flowers, and this was so unusual it was in the papers. I have seen the papers because my mother keeps them in a box and she shows them to me on special occasions. Josie had a broken hip from the motorbike and some money compensation. She says the hip was not as unbearably painful as having the baby (that is, me). But I couldn't help that, so it is not my fault really. When I ask her what it was like being in the papers and having your photo taken, she says it was a bore and that being a five-minute wonder is pointless. They never had their pictures in the paper again. They never had any other children either, because the accident spoilt my mother's equipment. They say they don't mind. They have me.

But I mind because I would have liked some brothers and sisters. Sometimes being an only child is not like being a child. Sometimes it's like not being there at all, and sometimes you are there too much.

They argued after I was born. My father did not like the name Shane. He said it was unsuitable for me. My mother wanted that name because of a cowboy in some film. My father liked the name Laurie, and in the end he won. But they never asked me. I know you can't exactly ask a baby, but it is still not fair. I hate my name. The other thing I hate is that we are always moving. My mother says I should blame my father because it is his job that makes us move all the time. Another thing they argue about is what kind of school I should go to. He wants me to get on with children from the area and go to the nearest school. She thinks I should go to a private school with a cap and a blazer and learn to talk more poshly. Josie was not born as posh as Brian. He uses long words a lot, and he explains them to me as he goes along, but she talks louder than him, and sometimes she sounds extremely posh. I don't care about being posh, but I hate moving all the time.

Now I am at another new school called Newlands Primary. When my father came to look round this school he brought me with him and we met the head teacher, Mr. Overson. I thought we were just going to say hallo, but suddenly Mr. Overson began testing me with questions.

~ How do you spell assassinate? How do you express two per cent as a decimal? What is the capital of Guatemala?

He thought I was backward because I couldn't answer any of these. My father sat there blinking. I wonder if even he knew the capital of Guatemala without looking in a book. When Mr. Overson said he would start me off in Miss Glennie's class with the ten-year-olds, Brian still said

11

nothing. Sometimes he forgets my actual age. So I started another new school with everyone thinking I am thick.

There is this boy in my class called Michael but everyone calls him Micka. He is smaller than me (well, nearly everyone is), and skinnier and his hair is a pale sickly red, like a dead leaf when it is rotting in a drain. His arm is as thin as a stick, the kind you could break by jumping on when you are making a bonfire. But his face is like an old wrinkled man's. I think it is because he is hard. One of his brothers is in prison. His uncle is a famous murderer. A girl told me this the very first day I was there.

This boy is absolutely from the area. He is lucky really that he can fit in without any trouble. He has a rough accent, rougher than all the rest of them, but they don't laugh at him.

I knew after only a few days that I didn't like this school or the other kids. Or the teachers. My father says of course I could fit in if I tried a bit harder. My mother says that being a child is just something you have to go through and it can't be worse than her childhood. She came from a big family and they all had to share bedrooms and even beds if they were the youngest. She did not come from Hertfordshire, where I was born, but from the West Country. Her family was poor but my father's family was rich. He married her because he felt sorry for her only having one coat. He has three coats and she has even more than that, suits and jackets and hundreds of clothes, more than anyone could wear I would say, even if she wore a different thing every day of the year.

But maybe that is why they were unhappy. They had too many things to fight over; my name, and the coats and jackets and sweaters, and the car my mother crashed once, and other things they thought I could not hear or understand. Then it came to the day after I had started my new school.

I am in my bedroom trying out one of my ideas, which is to cut a lemon pip and an apple pip in two and somehow glue them together to make a new species of tree. You have to make the pips mate. I know about mating, this is one of the things my father explained very clearly when we saw some cats stuck together making weird noises which I wanted to watch, but he disagreed because he said it is not the sort of thing you should stare at in public. I was only six then and he gave me exactly the right books about human and animal biology and said I was to ask him if I had any questions or was worried about anything. There are plenty of things I worry about, but I am not such a baby as to tell him. Which is one of the reasons why I have started to write some thoughts down in this log book.

I am putting the half pips together and I am just about to carefully wrap them in toilet paper while I think how to glue them when they come into my room without even knocking, looking serious as if I have done something terrible. They pull me to the bed and we all sit down in a row. Brian is holding my arm and Josie is squeezing my knees and we are all looking at the wall of my room where there is nothing to see because I haven't even had time to put any posters up. I wriggle, but I can't see their faces properly so I stop wriggling and wait. Brian does a kind of quiet coughing which means 'listen to me' so I listen, but at the same time Josie starts talking so I am hearing different things in both ears and it doesn't make a lot of sense – but this must be important because they are both very serious and my mother is even shaking a bit as if she is nervous, or maybe excited. I can never tell with her. They are holding me so tight it makes my skin itch and when they start talking, they go on and on like this for ages:

~ Mummy and I will be separating in two days' time . . .

~ That means Daddy will be living somewhere else . . .

~ Initially, in university accommodation . . .

~ And we'll both take you out for treats on your birthday . . .

~ And other occasions or seasonal celebrations, for example, Christmas . . .

Brian coughs again and looks at his shoes.

~ Your mother and I have decided, after a great deal of thought, that this is a civilised arrangement and therefore the best option for us all.

~ Laurie? Is everything okay? says Josie, trying to stroke my hair. I push her hand away.

What am I supposed to say? They are both looking at me now. If it's not okay, will that make any difference? I just want them to go away now. My lemon–apple pip tree is going to die if I don't give it some water quickly. They don't care about my experiment; all they want is to tell me their news and get it over with.

I say, Will I get two sets of presents this Christmas? Brian shakes his head and makes a tutting noise.

~ That is what is known as a mercenary attitude. Mercenary, meaning—

My mother hisses back at him like a mamba snake.

~ Don't be so stupid, Brian! He's only eleven! That was the first thing that popped into his head—

~ Take a moment, Laurie. Clear your mind. Remember to be logical and reasonable.

But I can't. I feel stupid and babyish.

~ Where will my home be now? My actual home? Do I have two bedrooms? Two beds? Two sets of clothes? Suppose they get mixed up by mistake?

My mother laughs and Brian sort of smiles. Have I made a joke?

~ Darling! What funny questions! It will be like going on holiday when you visit Daddy. You take a weekend bag.

~ We have every confidence in you, Laurence. You will soon get used to the new routine.

Now I know how serious this is, because he uses my full name. They look down at me. Waiting for what? They are still holding me so tight I breathe their breaths and I want to kick my legs free, but I can't.

~ What about mating?

They both jump at the same time as if I have stuck pins through their hands, and I feel I am going to giggle. So to stop it, I do a thing to my mouth that hurts, but they don't even know I am doing it. They are both staring at me, then over my head at each other. I wonder if this question is something they have forgotten when they decided to separate.

~ I mean, what about you two mating? Brian says you can't have marriage without it.

They both start speaking quickly at the same time, as if they are in a speaking race. My father says, That question is highly irrelevant to this discussion, at the same time as Josie is saying, Well, I think our little boy just hit the nail on the head . . .

They talk some more, but I don't remember it. They let go of me after a while and say good night and do I want a drink of water or anything? And my mother kisses me goodnight as if nothing has really happened.

I go back to my experiment. The lemon and apple pips

16

have gone all brown. Now I have cut them open they are never going to make a new tree. It was a stupid idea anyway.

Laurie. Is he a bully? He does not do it the same like my brother Lee. First he makes you like him then he hurts you then he says he is sorry then he buys something for you and makes you like him again. He has got long hair but he is strong. When I grab his hair and pull it he kicks my balls to death.

I can bear pain all right, but he can take more. We tested with matches on our thumbnails and said ready steady go and counted the seconds and I could bear it for seven seconds and he could bear it for ten. The others have respect for him because he is the biggest in class.

He has wrote his name for me. You don't write lorry. If you crack a joke on his name he gives you hell. Laurie is it. I have to get it right.

The pup Zak is a bad pup. He bites every time. When I give him the milk or some bread he bites my hand good and deep with his teeth like needles. He has to learn to bite soft when it is me. I have tried to train him gently like, but he won't obey his master. And he shits on my clothes and Mam will belt me if she finds out. But if you squeeze his face up he stops making his noise. You have to squeeze real hard, till your hands are hurting.

So it was nearly Christmas. I went to look at the shops in Walker Street. It is like being a ghost and treading in the streets of heaven. There is white everywhere, pretend snow on the starry lights and cotton stuff stuck on the windows and white spray stuff with glitter in it and all this white makes you forget to see the dirty bits of the street.

I watched the window with Snow White and the Seven Dwarfs moving. It is only machines but it looks more like real if you shut your eyes a bit. Snow White looks dead real. Her smile is all soft like Mam when she drinks whiskey and we have the fire on and she sits by it with the orange of the gas flames shining over her. Snow White with a blue dress and black plum hair, spun out from her face, stiff like black candy floss. And she keeps on waving to the dwarfs, and a tinny voice sings hello, come in. And they move in and shove presents in her arms, all done up smart in boxes with paper and silver stars and bows and all. All the boxes the same shape. Different colours of paper on.

Laurie says there is nothing inside the boxes but that is a lie. How does he know so much anyway? Laurie doesn't think much to Walker Street shops so we went to Findlay Street Shopping Centre and we went right inside the best shop. Galloways, it is called. Saw the little kids like, with their Mams in a line to see Santa. Some crying. Scared of Santa in the Grotto, in the dark, and he sits in there with a beard and he pulls you on his lap and he is whispering all the time. Mams

18

and Dads making them go in and then they came out with boxes all the same, wrapped like the dwarfs' boxes. They were smiling after they got their presents, and the Mams wiped their faces and said brave boy, good girl.

I would not cry in the Grotto even if it was pitch black and if Santa asked what do I want, I would say a kennel for the pup. The shitty pup has wrecked the box and chewed my clothes and still Mam and Kevo don't know he is there. But the stink is getting so bad I have to do something. He is getting quieter with the training and all; he does not bite so much but lies still. He is a skinny pup and he sleeps a lot. This will build his strength for when he gets bigger. He is a dirty pup and this is bad. But I have trained him as good as I can.

I asked Mam could I see Santa but she said I am too big for that. She has got a job in a pub. Maybe she will get me a present this year. Kevo says he will get me an airgun and teach me how to aim it at next door's telly.

Yesterday Mam was sick in the toilet. I heard her when I was in bed. Sometimes when she is sick I hold her hand but there is no room in the toilet to stand next to her. I made her some tea but she let it get cold. She said I was a good boy. Now Gran is away she hardly talks. Even with the whiskey it is just drink and sit and cry sometimes. She does the same if I am there or not there.

I want to give her a real good present for Christmas so

maybe I will go back to school this week to make something in the craft lesson. It is all free because they give you the card and the paints and they even have goldy stuff for angels and the teacher will help you if you can't decide. If I go back I will get in trouble because of wagging off but I can tell them Mam is sick. This time it is true.

Laurie showed me a thing to do with the pup. He got the pup outside and tied him to the fence. Pup trying to bite all the time. Laurie got a safety pin and stuck it through the pup's skin at his neck, in a little bit then out again. Did up the pin. Laurie said, Your pup's body pierced, he's real cool. Laughed.

The pup did not squeal. He turned round and round with his head to try and see what was in his neck. Laurie gave me a pin and showed me what to do. If it hurt bad the pup would growl. He said I could do the pup a nose ring with another pin if I wasn't scared.

I untied the pup and he was growling then. Laurie says I am feeding him wrong. Milk is no good because he is not a baby any more. He says to call him Brock. It is a good name. Laurie says Brock needs meat. Maybe I should ask Mam.

The pup, I mean Brock, would not go in the flat any more so I tied him up under the stairs. It is dark there and okay for him not to be seen if we are lucky. He is better there because of the shit.

Mam does not want Christmas. But I have made her a

card with a gold angel on. It says Happy Christmas from your little angel. The words were Miss Glennie's idea. I will give it to Mam on Christmas Day after Santa comes.

Lee has sent a card with a skull and bones on it to Kevo. He says to tell Mam he is coming home soon. He is in Strangeways. Sometimes he says he is coming back and he stays away. Maybe it will be a long time before he comes. Maybe something will happen and he won't come.

Kevo has got a job with Christmas trees. I asked would he take me to the shop with him. But they aren't in a shop, only by the road. He says he will bring us a tree on Christmas Eve. I don't remember if we had one before. Last year in the hostel there was one but it wasn't ours. Barbara and Denise the hostel ladies put presents on but they weren't real. We got wrong if we touched it. I broke the lights and Mam slapped me and she had to pay the hostel for the lights mending. But it was okay on Christmas Day when we got a good dinner and all of us kids played games and some presents were under the tree and this time they were real ones. I got a plastic car transformer from Santa. Mam got bath cubes and soap. Kevo got a pen with a mermaid on it; when you shake it her shells and tail comes on and off. Lee never stayed in that hostel, he was away.

Maybe Gran will come back. She is a good cook. She says you must always have a good dinner and a good break-fast. Mam is shite for cooking, she always sends me for chips.

I asked her about a turkey and gravy and she said, we'll see.

I know what that means.

At last there has been something quite good happening at my babyish new school. We had a social history lesson, and Miss Glennie told us about boy chimney sweeps. She has got a book like the books in my father's study (only his are thicker and the writing is much much smaller), and I think books like that are probably about a hundred years old. She reads a bit out of this book and then we talk about it. She was reading today about the way of training a climbing boy, which is what they used to call the sweeps' boys; how to wash their knees in salty water and scrub their knees with a hard brush every day, so no matter how much they scrape inside the chimney it will not hurt. It does at first, of course. In those days their trousers went into rags quite quickly, so they cut themselves on the stones of the chimneys.

When it was the time for the whole class to discuss this, I was the first one to ask things.

~ Did they bleed a lot? How did the sweep find the boys when they had finished? Did the boys die? Were they my size? Why did they climb if it hurt?

Miss Glennie said other people should have a chance to ask questions. Micka said he would have run away.

~ But, Michael, Miss Glennie said in her kind and soft voice, these poor boys had no choice. For them, it was work or starve. Sometimes it was their own fathers who were the sweeps and they beat them to make them climb higher.

I asked again, Why did they climb if it hurt and their knees were bleeding like you said? Why didn't they come down again?

Miss Glennie opened her eyes wide.

~ The sweeps would *light a fire in the grate of the chimney* when the boys were up, to make them go faster. They would breathe the smoke and get scared of choking. So the boys would climb quickly to the top so they could breathe the fresh air. Sometimes the smoke made them too dizzy to hold on any longer, and they let go and fell into the fire.

~ Why didn't their mothers come and save them? Lisa Carmichael asked that. What a stupid question to ask; such a girl question. All the other girls looked as if they were going to be sick. Miss Glennie's voice got very sad and she said, Very often they were orphans. They didn't have mothers.

Now, that is what I call a good lesson. If every day was like that I would be at school more often. But it was ruined by Miss Glennie making us do some writing about 'I am a climbing boy (or girl, even though girls did not do it but at school we must always say girls can do anything boys can do, even if it is something cruel that hurts, like climbing chimneys) and what are *my feelings* about chimney sweeping.' This could have ruined a brilliant lesson, except I didn't do the writing, just a kind of a cartoon picture of a sweep lighting a huge fire with a most evil grin on his wicked face, and in the next picture a little skinny boy climbing up and up, with a balloon coming out of his mouth saying, 'Can't breathe, choking, cough cough.' The boy looked like Micka. I showed it to him but he said my drawing was shite. Miss Glennie gave me a green star for the picture (of course), but she put underneath, 'Where is your writing, Laurie?' She is way too soft. A proper teacher would have torn up the picture and kept me in as a punishment.

Times I don't like Laurie like when his eyes go funny, they did this in the lesson about sweeps. He was breathing fast like after running a race. His mouth opens, it is all red inside like a fox. I don't say this, or he would say poof and girly, and fuck off. I did a drawing of him that was a fox body with a Laurie face. He likes this picture so I gave it him to keep.

At Christmas he is going away with his Dad. They are going to a five-star hotel. His Dad will let him drink vodka and champagne. On Christmas Day he is going to get a cigar.

My brother Lee is back. He has got a new belt. Kevo

brought home the Christmas tree and Mam got some snow stuff to put on it. I think she is not sick any more.

The pup is dead. Its paws were all chewed off. It did not last as long as the kitten. I think pups are more hard work than cats. And they stink a lot worse. Mam smelt the smell by the stairs and she found the box out there but it was empty. I put the pup in the bins real fast so she would not know. The box was wet and shitty but Mam saw my clothes in it. She pulled my arm behind my back and dragged me out to the stairs.

~ Is this yours?

~ No.

She clouted me, she kicked the box and she yelled.

~ It's not mine, it's Saeed's.

Saeed lives in the next flat. They don't have a Christmas tree but they get presents. His dad has a shop.

~ You pigging little liar, he's not allowed to have pets. What in Jesus' name was in here, it smells like dead rats . . . .

I got away from her and ran up the stairs and shouted down at her.

~ You should know what dead rats smells like . . .

She tried to catch me but I was way too quick, up the stairs along the landing then I could hear her moaning again. She stopped and went away to have a fag and get sick maybe.

I went out. I went to Walker Street and when I got to the Snow White window, I stood for a bit leaning up against the glass. Didn't look in the window; it was too white and frosty glitter everywhere. Even the street was too white to look. I was leaning against the glass with my eyes shut, thinking colours. Dark ones, dull like when the drain is clogging with dead leaves all slimy and black and green. Then a hand was shaking my shoulder, and I thought it was the shop man come to see me off for leaning on his window. I opened my eyes. There was this woman holding my sleeve. I shoved her off. She held out her hand to me. Didn't say nothing. A note was in her hand. She held it to me. Touched it to my hand. I grabbed the note and ran off. I ran and ran until I hurt to breathe. The money in a bunch in my hand. Then I took a good look at it and it was a fucking five pound note. I never had five pounds in my hand of my own before.

I smelt it good. It smelled like shit and metal.

I spit on it for luck. Kissed it like they do in the movies.

I wished Laurie was there to see, but not to tell me what to get. Buying is better than nicking. You can take your time buying. I could buy a thing for Mam now, for her Christmas.

I looked for ladies' things. In Galloways. Handbags. Gloves. Tights. Softy big scarves. Hats. Perfume. By the perfume counter, the smell was so heavy I felt it pressing on my clothes, going through to my skin. I looked for someone to ask, someone like Mam. But they all looked away; they closed their blue makeup eyelids and folded up their arms. Their nails were all sharp painted tiger claws red with blood. Their lips red like they had been dipped in wet blood.

I stayed too long in the one place, touched too many things. They called a man to throw me out, I showed him the money and he laughed.

~ Know what that is? Real leather that is, twenty pounds that purse is, nothing under a tenner here, nothing for the likes of you. Haway, piss off.

What is the point of five pounds? I looked at guns outside the gun shop. Kevo wants a gun. Five pounds is only worth shit.

What would Laurie do?

He would not get presents. He would buy a plane ticket and escape. He would buy fags for himself.

I bought sweets. You can get a load of sweets all right for five pounds. I stuffed them inside my shirt and they made a fat belly. I went back to the Snow White window in Walker Street and I watched people and I ate sweets. People pushed and shoved past. A little kid stopped and stared at me eating sweets. I chewed at her. Her dad pulled at her arm, pulled her away. I ate some more. It was late. I got sick.

I went out of Walker Street and found a quiet place down an alley and sat on a step. Waited to be sick. I thought about my dream of the fish with its blue eyes and the look it gave me always in the dream and the voice of it. The sick came easier then. I was cold after. I shook. I wiped the stuff off my face and some tears came. I never cry. The tears slid out by themselves.

I want some things for Christmas. Like I see on telly or in the shops or anything.

I don't care though. So long as Lee and Kevo don't fight and they don't belt me and Mam doesn't cry and we have a good dinner, not chips and burgers.

When I came back home the pup's box was gone. That was Christmas Eve. The electric was off. Mam had lit a candle. With the tree and all it was okay, but tomorrow there'll be fights and we won't have a good dinner. At the hostel we had turkey and crackers.

Kevo was home and he had a few cans and he sang Christmas carols, but not like Miss Glennie's singing. Like carols were dirty. He was in a good mood though. Then he went out.

Then Mam said to me, Michael, come here while I tell you. We're going to have a new baby . . .

~ What for, like?

How can she have a baby and her so old and sick all the time? Her face tries a smile for me, but all that's there is sadness and being tired.

~ Maybe a little sister for you . . .

~ Is Daddy coming back then?

The smile goes from her face. Don't ask me questions. Get to bed now. Be a good boy.

In bed I am cold. If I was to punch her belly she would talk. Lee would do that. He doesn't take shit from her. Kevo shouts till she cries and he slams the door and her hand shakes. All I do is fetch her fags and make her tea. Good boy. Go to bed. Once I kicked her chair and she slapped me. Only the once. Not hard either.

She looks different now. The baby makes her look like that.

A baby brother, crying in my bedroom.

Like the pup, shitting and squealing.

Not like Baby Jesus. Not like Christmas.

Mam will be in bed and no more shopping. Lee will cash her giro. It will all get spent the same day.

Later, I am asleep and Kevo falls in the bed and breaks my sleep. Breathing loud and a smell coming off him like when I got sick in the alley, a sweet smell of the drink coming off him; he always lays all over the bed with his clothes still on. He pushes me to the wall and I feel the cold wall pressing my side. Kevo sticks his knees up and pulls the covers off me. He is not asleep. He lies tight, bunched up to jump if the door is hammered. He can be out the window and drop two floors down before I even wake up.

~ Kevo?

~ Merry bollocking Christmas, now shut it . . .

~ Did you know about Mam's baby?

~ Yeh, stupid cow.

~ I didn't know. No one said.

29

~ Did you not notice the size of her? Fucking elephant.

~ But when's it coming? Soon?

~ Don't think about it. Most likely it'll end up like the other one.

~ What one?

Kevo turned over and over in the bed and punched the pillow and pushed me to the wall.

~ Before you, like. It died, poor little cunt.

~ What was it called?

~ Kevo got up and threw open the window.

~ Some Irish saint's name. Jesus Christ, it stinks in here.

~ A girl, was she? How did she die? How old was she?

~ You're a nosy little fucker. Why don't you shut it?

~ But, Kevo—

~ Stupid cow, at her fucking age . . . And he lays down again and soon he will be asleep with no cares about anything.

~ Is Daddy coming back?

~ What?

~ Where did the baby come from? Who's the daddy?

He grabs my leg and pinches hard.

~ How should I know? Go to sleep.

He pinches again, high up my leg by my balls. He pushes me to the wall. Cold against my side.

Kevo is asleep.

*

30

Black would be the colour if I would paint my Christmas, not black soft like velvet or shiny like Snow White's hair, but dry black, flat black like the soot stuff on old Babs' kettle.

When I woke up there was nothing from Santy. I looked around and around the room for a present. Even under the bed and under Kevo.

Lee was in the kitchen and when he sees me he starts. The belt is off and he's wrapping it around his hand. First thing, before we even sit down to breakfast. Mam says, Lads, let's have a bit of peace round here now. Remember the day that's in it.

Lee lets the belt slowly swing from his hand backwards and forwards and the buckle is a head of a wolf with fangs and it drops on the table by me.

~ Fucking Merry Christmas one and fucking all.

I say, real quiet like, Why did you come back?

He says to me dead soft, None of your fucking cheek, my son.

~ I'm never your son.

Mam shouts at me to shut up. Lee hits the belt buckle on the table and sends the milk flying, Mam screams, Kevo wakes up and comes in the kitchen. Sees Lee.

~ Home for Christmas are ye, you daft bugger?

Lee whispers to Kevo and they laugh. Mam makes toast and she gives me a present. It is a square flat thing wrapped in blue paper with stars.

31

~ Sorry, son, it isn't much; best I could do. She holds out her arms to me. I go to kiss her but Lee pulls my hair.

~ Soft as shite.

~ Why man, let him go, he's only ten, Kevo says. He is in a good mood, he has some cans opened already. I kiss Mam and she holds me to her and I feel her heart beating fast and she catches her breath and lets me go.

They all watch me opening my present. It is a book. Lee laughs.

~ New and all! Where d'ye nick that, Maureen?

Mam says he is not to call her Maureen. Kevo does not laugh. He lights a fag.

~ Come here and show us, Micka. Is it good?

It is a book for how to bring up a pup. It has pictures, good boys and girls brushing their pups. The pups are fluffy and they do not bite or shit like Brock. I wish Brock was not dead.

~ This is shite, Lee shouts out of nowhere, teaching him to rear pups from a fucking book. Real life is how you learn. *Real life*. He shouts it in my face. Kevo never says nothing. He does not stand up to Lee.

I go to the bedroom and Kevo follows me, comes in. I look for the thing I made Mam at school. Kevo waits, standing looking out the window.

~ That's a nice thing there.

~ It's for Mam.

~ Very nice. Here.

He gives me a new watch. Straps it on.

~ Happy Christmas.

I am not to tell Lee about the watch. Kevo does not say this but I am not to tell.

We go back to the room. I give Mam her present. It is a gold crown with all glitter and stars on it, as many as I could stick. Most have stayed on. Miss Glennie said it was good. Mam stares and stares at the crown. Lee says, Put it on then, you're the only queen here. Mam slowly, slowly puts it on. It is too big but she holds it with one hand.

~ Michael. That's a lovely thing you made me. Thanks, son.

Mam grabs me and squeezes me to her so I smell her face and her powdery smell under her nightie. She kisses me, then I get away and she rolls a fag still with the crown on her head and we laugh. Maybe that was not so black that time. But just after it got black all right. Lee put his can on the floor and I kicked it over. I never saw it there, I never meant to do it.

Lee is worst when he doesn't shout. I see him take the belt off and start to wrap it around his hand, still with the fag in his mouth. He says dead soft, Stand still, my son.

Mam is up out of her chair, and pushing me out of the room.

~ Get in the toilet, son, lock the door, we'll sort this out, it'll be all right, you'll see. Her crown is falling off and she lets it fall.

Lee is roaring. Kevo goes out. He won't stand up to Lee. Mam calls him not to go. But he goes.

I hear the slap of the belt on the kitchen table. Mam talking, pleading like. Lee laughing. I hate this time. I hate Lee. I hate Mam. And the baby that's coming.

Lee kicks the toilet door. Whacks at the handle with the belt buckle and the noise is so quick and loud I feel the piss jump out of my prick all by itself.

~ Come on out of there.

~ Fuck off.

~ You are fucking dead, my son.

~ Mam!

~ She's gone.

~ Mam, are you there?

~ Come out before I break the fucking door in . . .

He will too. Lee doesn't care this is our home, he doesn't care they told us at the hostel we are on our last chance. He is going to kill me. Mam is a long way away, sobbing. I am so scared I even wish our Da was back.

Then there is hammering at the front door. Police. Lee has his face pushed up against the toilet door. He whispers to me, If Kevo called them bastards he's dead, after I've done with you.

~ Open up!

I think Lee grabs Mam. He likes to twist arms, maybe that

34

is what he does. Mam is dead quiet. I put my ear to the door for Lee's whisper.

~ Open up in there!

~ Maureen, I'm warning you—

~ Let me go! I'm not one of your slags, I'm your mother, for God's sake; have you no respect at all?

~ If you don't open this door we'll break it down . . .

Lee is beaten. He hates that the worst thing. I hear Mam opening the front door. He says to me through the locked door, If you get me in shite for this, you'll pay for it. If she shops me, I'll cut out her fucking tongue.

I put my hand over my face and squeeze like with the pup. It is hard to breathe. I am not crying, there is water coming out of my eyes, but it is not crying if you keep quiet.

Then the police is in and Mam is telling them something like I am locked in the toilet. They knock on the door.

~ What's his name, Michael? Come on out of there, Michael. Come on, lad.

I open the door. Lee's belt has disappeared by magic. He has a greasy smile on, he pats me on the head. Mam does a fake laugh for the police. There are two there. One looks at me. One looks at Lee, up and down, up and down.

~ I'll check this lock for you.

The police is checking the lock. Lee is looking at me, Mam is looking at me. I have this lump of stuff in my chest, this hard thing hurts all the way up to my throat. My jeans are wet. I am crying. Mam holds me. Lee folds his arms and stares at me. Warning me.

~ We had a complaint of noise . . .

~ Sorry, officer, Mam says, stroking my hair, Christmas and all, we might have got a bit merry . . .

The police stops looking at the door lock.

~ Said it sounded like someone was being hit. Did anyone hit you, Michael?

~ No.

I see Lee nod. Saying no is the right thing. We must not shop Lee, he is family.

~ We're grand, thanks be to God, Mam says.

Old cop gives me a paper tissue to wipe my face.

~ They must have made a mistake, Mam says.

~ We're in the neighbourhood. If we hear any more complaints we'll be round again, he says to Lee. Lee is grinning back. Not a care in the world now.

They go away down the corridor. Mam says, Show the officers out, Michael.

By the door the young one stops.

~ Here.

He gets a shiny thing from his uniform pocket and gives it me.

~ It's a harmonica. You can play canny tunes on it.

The older one shakes his head: Haway, man, don't waste your breath.

36

Young one bends down and whispers.

~ Happy Christmas, bonny lad.

They are gone.

Inside me is something tearing. It tears as easy as wet paper.

My mother has an unusual method with the answer machine. I did not know you could use it to stop people talking to you when you are home. Sometimes she lets it ring and ring, and if it was me I would pick it up and at least say I don't want to speak to you, but she has no fear of anyone or anything. Sometimes she is not even doing anything important, maybe painting her fingernails or watching telly or just staring into the air and she waves her hand at me when I go to pick it up and waves me down into my chair again. Of course I am not scared of her, and I could pick it up if I wanted to, but at the moment it is an interesting experiment to leave people, like she says, stewing in their own juice.

And anyway, when she is asleep or not there I can listen to all the messages. And if I feel like it I can even erase them. She does not know I know how to do this, but it's actually simple. Easier than working the video, but she thinks that's difficult too. She would not learn when my father wanted to teach us, so only I learnt.

My father is the one who most often leaves messages on the machine. Some of them are funny, because he has no idea we are sitting there listening to him. Josie makes rude faces while he is talking. If she was at school she would be getting into big trouble for her behaviour. Some messages seem sort of sad. But she says it is ridiculous to feel sorry for him, he is not sad at all, he just sounds sad because he has drunk some vodka first, to give himself Dutch courage to phone. She seems to know all about how he is getting on, even though she does not live with him any more. Sometimes he calls and leaves a message when he is irritated. He never ever gets angry, only irritated. He told me this himself, so it must be true. He said that people like him don't get angry, it shows a lack of self-control. I think he is absolutely right and I will try to be like him, because I think fearless people never get angry.

I think I am adjusting very well to the new way things are. It is really easier when people do not talk to each other. I have questions sometimes, but if I am really clever I am sure I won't need Brian and Josie to work out the answers.

Do they ever talk about me? Maybe I am one of the reasons why they had to separate. What do they really think about the new arrangements? Do they ever wish they could go back to how things were? What does the left out one do with themselves when I am not there?

My father's messages are never about me. They are usually about collecting things he has left in our house. Or about how he is kept waiting when my mother forgets the arrangements she has made. And financial settlements.

My mother does not seem to need anything. Sometimes when I come in from school she is sitting just where she was when I went out, and she has not done any shopping or anything, and she does not mind how untidy things are. I suppose she is showing self-control.

Soon my father will collect me for his part of the holiday. His suits used to hang in the cupboard. My mother has left the empty spaces where his things used to be. Who made the rule that she stays in this house and he goes? Who made the rule that I must have half Christmas Day with her and half with him? Will they ask me one day what I think about these civilised arrangements?

CHAPTER 2

1995, January

I put the telephone down in the hotel room. My father was pouring more vodka into his glass.

~ Can I have some?

~ How was your mother?

~ Can I taste some of your vodka?

He looked at me as if I was a bad dream. Then he shook his head more than once. When he stopped shaking, I was still there though.

~ Ten years of age is too young to begin—

~ Just a taste. It's Christmas. And I'm eleven. Go on, just a bit from your glass?

~ Did your mother give you any message for me?

~ Yes, she said to let me have some vodka.

He breathed in and out a few times extra loudly, looking up at the ceiling. This is a way of showing he is irritated without him having to say anything. Sometimes my mother does an imitation of this to make me laugh, which is what I was remembering. He stood up suddenly.

~ I think we had better open our presents now.

He got on a wobbly hotel chair very slowly and still holding his glass. He reached up with one hand and took a parcel off the top of the wardrobe.

~ Stand here, Laurence, and I will pass it down to you.

I knew it was up there, ever since we unpacked, even though he had pushed it to the back. I could have opened it millions of times since we arrived. He has got no idea about secrets. She is way better at secrets; when she hides things I have no idea where to look.

I got his present out of my bag which I had put under my bed. Josie had bought it for me to give him. She forgot to tell me what it was, but I know it was not expensive. It was a small present, not like the huge thing my father gave me. We opened them at the same time. His present from me was a cartridge pen. My present was a set of encyclopaedias, with long words and small writing. Grownup books, because he says I have an adult reading age.

~ Did you choose this? Extremely useful. Thank you.

He tried the pen out on the hotel fire regulations. It didn't work, but he said it probably would once the ink had come through. He bent over me and breathed vodka and orange on my cheek. Then he pushed out his lips without moving his head, to kiss my cheek. His lips were watery and they left a trail on my skin, like being kissed by a giant slug. I suppose he does not get any practice at kissing now. At least I only have to be kissed by him twice a year. (The other time is on my birthday.)

~ Dad, it isn't working because of the plastic stuff on that card.

He wasn't interested in the pen. He started opening the encyclopaedias and showing me how to look things up in the index. (Volume 10. A whole big book just for the index of the other nine!)

~ I considered whether to buy you an encyclopaedia on disc but all those programmes are designed by Americans and they are for much younger children. This is an adult encyclopaedia; an invaluable resource in years to come. Never forget that books are the only lasting way to store knowledge. Computer discs are ephemeral, which means they will deteriorate after a certain number of years. Books last several lifetimes.

He opened the index.

~ Look here, under 'A' you find aborigines, they are Australian indigenous peoples. Volume One.

I looked up aborigines in Volume One. I wanted to see if there were pictures of women with no clothes on. But it was actually better than that. There was a description of a ceremony . . .

~ This would appear to be an initiation ceremony for the young men . . .

They cut their pricks. It said it in the book. My father

let me read it. They make a cut down to the root, almost, and it changes the way you piss from a stream into a sprinkler. It did not say that in the book; I made that up.

~ Does it hurt?

~ I can only imagine the sensation would be excruciating.

We had a long talk about this. My father actually knows a lot if you ask him the right kind of questions. He is a professor, so he likes talking about stuff you only find in books. He said that one day we might go to Australia and even meet some of the tribes in the book and see some ceremonies for ourselves. When he talks about these kinds of things he is very calm and has no fear, which is the right way to be.

After we had gone to bed I could not sleep for hours. I wished we had things like that ceremony in this country. Things that test your endurance. I could think of some excellent tests. I have plenty of ideas.

My Gran is back from Aberdeen. She brought me a present, called Edinburgh Rock. She says my Uncle Mikey will be home soon so she has come back. Mam talked with her when Kevo and Lee were down the pub. Gran wants Mikey to live with us while he is out on sick leave. It won't be for long, she says. Mam does not want him here but he is very sick with the AIDS and we are his only family now. Mam is his sister.

My Gran is okay. She does not curse or get in a rage when Mam cries. The baby is coming in April. Gran had twelve babies but some died and one is in the navy. I never met them, only Uncle Mikey and Bernie and another auntie I can't remember her name, only her hair in brown ringlets the colour of a horse's mane. My Gran is Irish, like Mam but more Irish even. She sings the songs, but not when Lee is there. And she can talk in the language of it.

I told Gran about the pup. She said I should live in Clare and have a farm. When she was nine she had a donkey all her own and three chickens. And in the country the hills are all different colours and there was green moss on the roof of her house. She loves her whiskey. She and Mam drank the whole bottle down while Lee was out signing on. Kevo is signing on too; there is no work for him now Christmas is over. Mam needs things for the baby. Gran says she can tell it will be a girl.

I drew a picture for Gran; it was mostly green and blue, like her life. She wears a blue coat that smells of another country. She spilt some whiskey on the picture and she said, God forgive me. She gave me a kiss before I went to bed. She sleeps with Mam, in her bed. Uncle Mikey will sleep in Lee's room. Lee will sleep on the floor in the living room. If he stays.

*

44

It came to the third of January, which was the day my father had agreed to hand me back to my mother for the last part of the Christmas holiday. We had to get the train back from where the hotel was, in the country. I had had enough of the hotel and the country. I prefer towns because you can do more things on your own in towns.

We were supposed to meet her on the platform and my mother did not see us at first; she was looking past us to another man and boy. Even though it was cold enough to snow she was not wearing a coat. My father did not say hello or anything, just, Josie? You are under-dressed. Putting your health at risk.

~ What do you care, Brian?

~ Ssh, not in front of— Brian shielded one hand with the other so he could point at me without me seeing. But who else could he be talking about?

~ I never see you except with him so what else can I do?

~ Whose fault is that?

~ I thought you didn't want a scene.

~ And which of us sabotages the arrangements every time? Not me, *my dear*.

~ Laurie! Darling! Lovely to see you, did you have a good Christmas? I want to hear all about it.

She was ignoring my father. She bent down and squeezed me into her, and I felt how cold she was. My father watched and after a while he went away. He forgot to say goodbye to me.

~ Let's go home, darling. I have a *wonderful* surprise for you!

We took a taxi. The driver called me 'squire'. My mother thought that was funny.

Home had got a bit different. I suppose it started getting different after my father moved out, but I didn't notice it when I was there every day. Now I noticed. All the rooms were full of stuff. Some of it was in piles on the floor. There were a lot of newspapers in piles. My room was just the same as I left it, though. I have told Josie never to go in my room. There was a different kind of smell around the house. In the kitchen were stacks and stacks of dirty plates. My mother hates doing washing up. She was always asking my father for a dishwasher.

We went in the sitting room. There was an enormous shape in there with a blanket over it. My mother did a kind of a dance around it. She was very interested in this present.

~ Lift it up, darling. It's from me. Happy Christmas!

I lifted up the blanket. There was a huge glass tank. Lying in the bottom of it was a snake.

~ It's a reticulated python. Isn't he a magnificent brute?

The snake was asleep. I tapped on the glass to wake it up.

~ Are you pleased? I thought he would be just perfect for you.

My mother was staring at me as if I was the snake myself. She put her lips to my ear and hissed, You know what we eat? *We eat live rats!*

~ Where will I get live rats from?

She knew. She had done some research about this. She licked her lips and smiled at the sleeping snake in its cage.

~ We can buy live food at the shop where I bought him.

I think I would have enjoyed this if I had thought of it myself. It is the kind of idea I often have. Having a pet snake to obey my every command is good. But I don't think this is my snake; I think it is hers.

~ What are you going to call it? Look at his markings. What about Kaa, like the python in *The Jungle Book*?

~ *The Jungle Book* is crap.

~ You used to love it.

~ When I was six.

~ Well, what then?

~ He's my snake, isn't he? I don't want him to have a name.

~ I think you are being very childish, Laurie, she said rather loudly.

The snake woke up. Its eyes were yellow and it saw me and knew I was not scared of it at all. It stretched itself along the edge of the glass. First I thought about taking it out and holding it. There was quite a lot of it. So then I thought I would wait until it knew me better.

~ Feeding time, said Josie. She was looking at me and smiling in a rather infuriating way. She stroked her hand along the glass where the snake was. I was absolutely certain she had already taken the snake out of the cage and held it. I knew she wanted to do it again, showing off to me. I knew that if I let her, she would take over the snake and the live rats and the power of it.

~ Do you want to feed your nameless snake, Laurie, or shall I do it for you?

~ I'll do it. Have you got any . . . food here already?

My mother put her cold hand on my shoulder and pulled me with her.

~ Oh yes. Come and see what's in the kitchen.

Later on I was reading about boy chimney sweeps in my encyclopaedia, but it is not as well done as the aborigine things. I was in bed and the telephone rang downstairs. It must have rung about twenty times. My mother did not answer it. Then it started ringing again straight away. I got up and went downstairs to find her. She was in the sitting room watching the snake. She was wearing her dressing gown.

~ Shall I answer it?

~ No. Leave it.

~ I can't leave it; it's keeping me awake.

~ Oh, don't fuss, Laurie. It's only your father.

~ Maybe he wants to speak to me.

~ What, at half-past eleven at night?

~ Why won't you answer it?

~ There. It's stopped now.

She put on the answer machine.

~ Are you happy now? He can leave a message for you and you can ring him tomorrow.

She put her hand into the snake cage and stroked the snake. It was not asleep. My mother has no fear of anything, which of course is good. But sometimes I wish she would do ordinary things like wearing coats when it's cold and answering the telephone. Now my father has gone, I can see how many ordinary things he used to do to save her the bother. Maybe she should get a job. That would make her more ordinary.

~ How many more days till school starts?

She suddenly pulled her hand out of the cage. She actually looked surprised.

~ I felt him squeeze my hand.

~ How many more days?

~ Put your hand in just here and feel him squeeze; it's a very strange sensation.

~ You remember about my school, don't you? Newlands Primary, with Miss Glennie, where I have to learn to get on with children from the area, like you said . . .

~ Oh, Laurie, don't fuss. It's only a school. Sometimes you—

~ I what?

~ You sound horribly like Brian. Fussing. Just relax.

I put my hand inside the cage. The snake bit me.

It's good that the holidays are over. Mam is real big now; she needs to lean on me when she gets up the stairs to our flat. If I stand next to her she leans on me with all her weight. Her legs are blue and knobby. Gran is always sending me back to the shops to buy fags and stuff Mam forgot. Gran is great on meals, she hates burgers; she buys proper butcher meat and makes stew like we get for school dinner. She says burgers and chips is not a good dinner for growing lads. They have dinners at school but sometimes Mam forgets to tell them and they take me off the free list. Mam does not write so good so she has to call down to the school and tell them. But now with the baby and all she can't walk to the school so easy, so she says she will make a pack lunch. It is okay while Gran is here, she turns on the fire real early and we can easy get warm. Kevo has robbed a load of carpet and nailed it to all the floors so it is warmer. That was Gran's idea. Lee has not been around much.

Some men came to mend the lift after New Year's Day. There was a fire in the lift New Year's Eve but it did not work before that. They left their tools in a bag on the fifth floor (not our floor). When they came back from buying fags their tools were gone. They said they wouldn't fix the lift. Gran went to the lift doors and screamed at them that there was a baby coming. Lee was reading a paper in the kitchen. He said he would do them over. Gran came back in the kitchen but Lee did not move. The men drove off. Maybe Lee robbed the tools. Him and Kevo had a big row over some money the next day; maybe that was the money for the tools. Lee is best at robbing but Kevo has the friends to sell things on.

If the police come round asking, it will be good if I am at school. Gran helped me make some New Year's resolutions, which are:

Get another pup, a good one this time.

Go to school every day.

Stand up to Laurie.

Help with the baby (Gran's idea). But I will if everything else goes right.

Get back at Lee for what he did on Christmas. That one I did not tell Gran. Why is it all the good people are tired and old and the bad ones are strong?

Last day of the holidays I went to Royts Lane to see were there any more pups, but not from the same old bitch as last time. This time I have the pup book and it will be different. Maybe Kevo will help me train the pup and Gran will give me proper meat to feed it.

I went looking around the site for Bluey. There was a Christmas tree with all the Christmas stuff still on it and the little kids were burning it. They have no coats. There was one girl called Minty gave me a thing off the tree. It was a sparkly bit of a moon. She had a smile and her snot was running into her mouth and she sucked it in. I asked how old she was but they did not know. She was sucking on the titty of a bottle. But they did not call her a baby like they do in our world.

I saw the back of Babs' old coat and she was walking to her trailer and I ran calling her. She turned and frowned and made strange with me. I asked for Blue and she squinched up her eye and looked out toward the road. She said he was away with the men buying a lorry.

She walked on and I went behind her and at her trailer she turned sudden, catching me with her eye.

~ Still there, gorgio boy?

She went in her trailer and I went after. She did not shout at me so I sat down. She put a plate on the table with bread and butter. She did not say I was to have it but I took a bit and she looked at me eating and let me eat. All the while she stood by the stove. She never sits in the trailer; Blue says she chokes in a place with a roof.

Then she showed me the present he gave her for Christmas, it was a big gold cage with a parrot in it. Even if you look right close up, it looks like real. Its feathers are green, real mad green with bits of red that makes the green look more

52

green. And it has a big beak, crooked and shiny black, and the eyes are black too, black glass. You can open the cage and put your hand in. Babs put it hanging outside her trailer. It looks more alive even in the outside light. The parrot's name is Geordie. She says she had a husband called Geordie once upon a time. When Babs laughs, I see all her black teeth at the back.

She said that Bluey goes around all the time with the men now, calling for scrap with the cart and the pony, and him only the same age I am. Babs said he is real good at coaxing the stuff from people, for all he's so young. That's how he got the parrot. Babs doesn't care it wasn't new. I wish there was good scrap around our flats, I am always looking by the rubbish bins but if there is ever anything, it goes as soon as you blink.

Babs was in a good mood then and I told her about the woman giving me a fiver on Christmas Eve. She said I should sing in Walker Street, she used to sing when she was young and it worked real good, better than straight monging, which is begging. I said I wasn't begging anyway, the woman just gave it me. She pinched her eye at me like I was a liar. Told me to sing her a song. I ran off then into the field next to the trailer site. I hid by a bush and from a long way off I saw her come into the field. I thought she was looking for me so I kept dead quiet. She squinched her eyes around and looked quick behind her, then she backed up to the hedge.

I had no time to move. It was like my eyes was glued open and stuck on the one place. She pulled up her dirty skirt and pulled down her knickers and squat down with her head twisted on one side. Her face was all screwed-up like, and she was sucking through her teeth like my Gran when she tries to thread a needle. I saw her shit come out of her saggy old bum and she went on groaning like it was hurting. I couldn't look away, it all happened too quick. She put her hand behind her back and down and wiped her bum with her hand. After, she drew that hand across the wet grass a few times and sniffed her fingers. She stood up, staggered like she might faint or fall and I prayed she wouldn't. I didn't want to pick her up out of her shit. She rubbed her face with the same hand she wiped her bum with. Then she took a long time to pull up her knickers and I could see her old legs with all their blotchings, blue and green and brown like a map of the world printed on her legs. She shook her skirt down to the ground and turned around and looked at her shit for a while, shaking her head.

After she was gone, I went to look. I never thought about how they do it. Living in trailers, that is what they have to do. They are free to come and go and wag off school, but they have to shit in a field.

Bluey as well. I will never eat anything from here again ever. If he has sweets he always gives me some. And once he made me a slice of bread and jam and held the slice in his hand out to me. Then when I thought of the bread and butter from Babs still in my belly I felt sick. I ran out of the field and along by the canal and the mud smelled like shit. Every time I shut my eyes I saw Babs' face all pinched up, and after, her shitty hand rubbing more black lines in her face.

I will go to school tomorrow. See Miss Glennie. She told us once she has a shower and a bath in her house. And when she wears a white dress, it is still white when she goes home.

So I went to school. Laurie says he had a great time at Christmas. His Dad let him get drunk. Vodka is no colour so his Dad did not know how much Laurie was putting in his Coke. And in the Coke you can hardly taste it, which Laurie says is good because it burns your mouth. He says he will give me some one day when I come to his Dad's. His Dad has just got a new flat in Barras Square, in the middle of town and at night you can watch out of the window, there are drunks roaring and falling over and getting kicked or nicked. It is better than his old house because his Dad has no car-pets or chairs so they have their dinner on the floor. I asked what about his Mam. But he walked away.

I stayed in school all day today; it was better than hanging round outside McDonalds in the cold. Laurie wants me to go with him to Royts Lane. He does not know how to get to it because it is not on any map written down. I don't want him to go there. Royts Lane is my place. He has enough places of his own. He says if I don't take him he will find his own way there. And he gives me such a look that I have to kick him under the table on the flat part of his knee and I make his cheeks blow out and his eyes go bulging like when you blow up a balloon. Miss Glennie sees us.

~ What's the matter, Laurie?

~ Nothing, Miss.

Laurie is cool. He never cries. He never tells. I wonder is he a real human sometimes.

I told Laurie about Mam's baby coming. He said it was gross. I asked why is it gross? He said having a baby is a pun-ishment for doing sex when you are not married, which is gross. I said my Mam was married. He said how did I know. He said sex was gross anyway. He knows because he has a huge book that tells him everything about sex with pictures and all. I asked could I see it. He said the same as always, One day. One day.

At break time Miss Glennie touched my sleeve of my shirt as I was going out.

~ Sorry, Miss, forgot my coat again . . .

~ No, it isn't about that, Michael. I want to have a word with you.

~ Miss, I've done nothing.

She laughed.

~ It's something nice. Something you would like.

I stood by her desk. Everyone else was in the playground. She was smiling at me. Talking to *me*. All her face so smooth, like she never went out in the rain, and her lipstick was gentle pink, like the colour lips should be, but not shiny wet like Lee's slags.

~ You know there's going to be a class outing this term?

~ No, Miss.

~ Well, there is. Are you pleased?

~ Yes, Miss.

I closed my ears then. I couldn't go, not in a million years would Mam let me go.

~ I would especially like *you* to come this year. Michael?

~ Okay, Miss.

I wished I was not there. I wished Miss Glennie was not talking to me specially. I wished I had wagged off.

~ I am taking our class to see a play called *The Little Prince*. It is a play with a ballet and music. The designer is a very famous man and the set and the costumes will be ... heavenly. You would love to see the colours and – oh, it will be just magical.

~ Okay, Miss.

~ Michael, don't look so miserable. I wanted to talk to you about this quietly, just the two of us, because I know things are not easy at home. About the money ... it won't cost you anything, you can tell your mother.

~ Okay, Miss.

~ And I will bring you back to your house afterwards, tell her. There isn't anything she has to do except say yes. Will you tell her?

~ Yes, Miss.

Miss Glennie's face went sad and she breathed out sadness.

~ Your art work is the best in the class. Does she know that?

~ Don't know, Miss.

~ Someone who has the ability you have ... don't you see, you should have this opportunity, however tough things are at home. How are things? At home.

~ Okay, Miss.

~ We are going to read the book about the Little Prince in class this term. It is a beautiful story. Sad, but beautiful.

~ Can I go now, Miss?

~ All right. No – wait. I'm going to write your mother a note. Please make sure she gets it.

Miss Glennie wrote a note in turquoise ink with a nib pen. I have just learnt that word, turquoise. The ink from those pens comes out shiny and wet and when it dries the colour goes paler, but it is still shiny. Teachers have things no other people have. Where is their world, I wonder.

~ There you are; put it in your schoolbag. If I haven't had an answer from her in a week's time, I will come round after school and ask her to sign the permission form. That's all she has to do, tell her.

~ Okay, Miss.

Miss Glennie in my house. Sitting in the kitchen with Mam and Lee and the cans and the belt and the whiskey. And the smell of the flat and the shouting and roaring and the lift broken and all. Miss Glennie cannot come in our world.

I gave Mam the note when she was on her own. Before I could even open my mouth to read it to her, she threw it in the bin.

~ Interfering cow.

~ It was only about the school trip. Can I go, Mam?

~ Can you in your dreams go? What with? We've no money.

~ Miss Glennie said it was free. Everyone else is going. It was in the note.

~ There'll be a catch; there always is. Don't trust them people, son. Kevo'll take you to the pictures if you want to go out.

~ I want to go, Mam. Can I go? She said it costs nothing and I have a star for my art work and I should go.

~ What's drawing pictures got to do with her? You can draw without her sending me letters. Does she think I don't know you can draw pictures?

~ Just sign a piece of paper. Anything. Please, Mam?

~ I'm tired. I'm going to bed. Here's 50p. Get yourself some chips.

~ That's not enough. Chips cost 75p.

~ Always wanting, always needing. You're driving me into an early grave.

Slowly she got up and went out the door, holding on to the table like she was drunk, but she had taken no drink. It was the baby making her so heavy she could not stand right. The baby driving her into an early grave. The baby coming.

I got Miss Glennie's note out of the bin. It was wet from the tea bags. The ink was pale and watery. A little frill of the turquoise writing at the edge. Turquoise, Mam doesn't know that colour. She can't read the words and she can't draw the pictures and she can't make good dinners but she can tell me can I go or can't I go.

I will go. Drive her to an early grave. I will go anyway.

Next day at school, it was playtime. Miss Glennie called me back.

~ Well, Michael?

~ Yes, she says I can go.

~ Oh, I'm so pleased. Did she sign the note I gave you? Have you brought it for me?

~ Shite – oh sorry, Miss. I left it at home, I'll bring it tomorrow.

I ran out the class and into the playground with the burning lump of stuff that comes in my chest sometimes. Right up to my neck and when I swallowed I felt it pressing my throat. I had to kick something real quick. There is a tree in the playground, an ugly dirty old tree with black branches and there is a cut in the side of it and it bleeds kind of a glue stuff. And when it has finished bleeding the tree will be dead.

I was kicking the tree. Mr. Overson the head caught hold of my shirt and he pulled me back, away from the tree and shouted I must come to his office. He kept hold of me and pulled me with him and slammed the door and stood tall over me and folded his arms. If I moved away even a little, his long arm shot out and pulled me back near him.

~ Look at you. Look at the state of you.

~ Yes, sir.

~ What do you think you were up to? *Answer me.*

~ Don't know, sir.

~ I saw you. Are we not to have any beauty in our lives – are we to live surrounded only by concrete and metal because it can't be torn or burnt or smashed or *kicked*? Are we?

~ Don't know, sir.

~ Come here.

Mr. Overson dragged me to the window and there was a good view of the tree all right.

~ I don't know why you were doing it, Michael, but you were kicking that tree. That is a live thing; that is a bloody sight more alive than you are. And it's more beautiful than you and I like it more than you. So that is why, if I find you kicking it again, you will be suspended for a week and I will personally come round and tell your mother why.

He held my face right up against the glass and made me look at the tree. Out of his window the branches rose up in the shape of a drop of water. I could not see that when I was down in the playground.

Mr. Overson gave me a shake and let go.

~ Have you anything to say?

~ No, sir.

~ Did you hear what I said?

~ Yes, sir.

I was nearly out the door and he turned from the window sudden like, and said, If there's any more trouble from you, you'll be barred from the outing. I'm warning you.

Laurie was not at school that day; he must have money. Then he goes to the machines in the arcade, not Findlay Street but the Penny Robbers in the alleys. He says there are men there give him money and he doesn't have to do anything for it. He has a life all right.

*

I have not kept my secret logbook enough this year. The reason is, it is much harder now I live in two places. Packing and getting on trains all the time means I don't have any time to think about ideas or experiments. On the train I usually think what I am going to say about one of them to the other one. I have to remember what I've said that's a lie, what one parent told me to tell the other parent that's a lie, and what I am not going to tell either of them at all, ever. I have found out that I am really excellent at lying. I did not know this before. I try to think like a soldier or a spy in France in the Second World War. I have been reading about the War a lot in my encyclopaedia. I have got bored with aborigines but I am looking around for a pointing bone. A pointing bone is what the aborigines used to kill people without having to touch them and there is no blood or any struggle. If you find the right bone and put the magic in, it will do everything for you and no one will know it is you who did the killing. It only works if you believe in it one hundred per cent. I will not make up my mind until I see that the bone has definitely worked. Then of course I will believe. And the more deaths it does, the more I will believe in it.

Micka's gypsy site must be a good place to find my pointing bone. They probably have some human bones stashed away somewhere.

Micka has got to be persuaded to take me there. He says

it's his place, not mine, and the gypsies don't want to have strangers coming on their territory. How come he is suddenly an expert? He has got a cold at the moment and he seems to be sniffing all the time and he wipes his snot on his sleeve or even his hand, and he never has any ideas for things to do when we wag off school, except for drawing. Glennie is madly in love with him; she calls him up to her desk all the time and he stands so close his snot nearly drips on her shoulder.

I never get colds and I am trying to become impervious to winter. This is what Brian says my mother is. How I do it is by taking off my coat and not wearing a vest, and if it rains I keep the hood of my jacket down and leave it open.

This morning it was raining. That cold kind of rain that should be snow. The wind was lashing it into my face, and after a while my forehead started to ache. The ache started on the outside, on my skin, and when that had got really frozen, the ache moved inside and went deeper into my head and my brain. It felt like the wind was whipping at me whatever direction I walked. My hair was soaking wet and it dripped down inside my shirt and the drips were like steel daggers sliding down my back. There is a Chinese torture with slow drips of water on your forehead, constantly and without ever stopping, until you go raving mad. If the water was ice cold, I think the torture would be even better. Thinking about Chinese torture was not enough to stop me thinking about the thing that keeps dripping into my brain like those water drops.

What is going on with Brian? Josie doesn't answer the messages he leaves for her. She still does not know I listen on the answer machine and then I press rewind so the message is all fresh for her to hear it, if she was bothered to. I think she often is not bothered at all. I don't blame her. If you have split up with your husband, you don't want to listen to his voice moaning on all the time. But I am sure he is trying to plot something and he needs her to agree. I don't know what it is, but it must be something to do with me.

His message last night said, The present arrangement has become entirely unsatisfactory. You must communicate. He has been kept down a year because of your neglect. If you would only agree on a compromise ...

What is a compromise? Has she promised him something?

Then I got to school. I looked at my face in the mirror in the girls' toilet to see if it was blue. It felt cold enough to be blue. It felt so cold I was sure that bit of me was dead. I wanted to see what a dead person's forehead would look like. I pushed my hair back and looked. The light in the girls' toilet is not very bright; it has a kind of metal cage thing over it. Even so, I did not look any different. Only my hair looked wet, that was all. My forehead was not even the slightest bit blue.

Suppose I ran away, would they get back together? Or what if I was dead, would Brian and Josie cry? Would they both come to my funeral, or would they have a row about who should be there? Perhaps they would not even feel anything. Impervious. How do you get to be like that? It would be good to be like that.

When I was in the bath last night, Josie came into the bathroom. She never even knocked or said can I come in. She was looking for her hair spray. Then she saw I was there and in the bath and she said, Sorry, darling. Have I embarrassed you?

~ I wish you'd knock. How would you like it if I came in when you were in the bath?

~ I wouldn't mind.

~ Yes, you would.

~ I wouldn't give a toss. When you were a baby we used to bath together. Don't you remember?

She came over to me and sat on the edge of the bath and she was smiling and kind of half-looking to see what she could see. I know I have never seen her in the bath. Or Brian.

I got the sponge and threw it at her full of water and it hit her in the chest. If she had been an ordinary mother she would have got angry and shouted, but she didn't. She started laughing and she was still looking at me under the water and she threw the sponge at me. She knew just where to throw it. It did not hurt, but all the time she was looking at me down there and laughing.

~ Have I made you angry?

~ Fuck off, Josie.

It was the first time I had said it to her out loud. But still she did not get angry. She stretched out her hand and she stroked my hair away from my face, and she licked her lips and her lipstick was all shiny.

~ What a man you'll be soon, Laurie.

Then she went away, and I didn't know if she was being serious or winding me up. It gave me a funny feeling, not knowing. I think mothers shouldn't make you feel like that.

CHAPTER 3

February

I was at the park with Laurie and we had a fight and I would not do what he wanted, which was catch one of the ducks. It is not my business to help him kill ducks and stuff. He is a liar and he never does what he says. He told me his mother is a tart but that is a lie. If it was true it would shame him to say it. So I know it is a lie.

So I went home and Uncle Mikey was there. I never saw him before. I knew it was him because of the scar he has on his face, it is shaped like a moon half full. Kevo told me how he got it.

He was sitting by the fire and the light not on, staring into the gas flames. Not even smoking a roll up.

~ Where's Mam and me Gran?

~ Out.

I sat down next him. He stared at the flames. Inside his nose I could see the wet and it shone in the light of the fire.

~ Uncle Mikey?

68

~ That's me.

~ Are you okay?

~ I don't complain.

His voice is like Gran's. When she showed me his photo he was brown-haired. Now his head is shaved close and the colour is silver and only his eyebrows are the same brown.

He never looked at me. His left hand went into a fist, then it opened up again and he shoved it in his pocket and pulled out his baccy and started rolling a fag. His fingers gentle with the paper, like it was a butterfly wing he didn't want to break. One hand shaking, the bad hand, the one that got mashed in the fight in the prison canteen. The small tube, he licked, he sealed, like a little stick the same both ends. Then whistled through his teeth, not true whistling, breathing more like.

~ Are you better?

He looked at me and he wasn't smiling.

~ Are you taking the piss?

~ I didn't mean anything . . . only Mam said you was sick.

~ I am.

~ You don't look so bad.

He lit the fag with a match. Rubbed the scar on his cheek with his good hand.

~ There's this boy at school and he showed me pictures of dead people and they were smiling.

~ There's worse things.

~ What things?

~ Things worse than dying. And some people are better off dead.

~ How? How are they better off?

~ You'd be doing them a favour. They fucken ask you for it. When you've done with them. Begging you.

~ Gran says you never meant to do it.

~ You know your trouble?

~ What?

~ You listen to yer ones too much. You mind that.

He smoked the fag down to the butt and threw it on the stone by the fire. 'Ones' is women. That is Irish. I wanted to ask him stuff, even if he was to hit me. But he's not like Lee; he's got more guts than Lee, Kevo says.

Uncle Mikey looked sideways at me and threw me a smile. So I asked, How did you get sick?

I thought, now I've done it. He'll kill me now and throw my bones on the ground for the dogs, like old Babs with the chickens at Royts Lane.

He stood up and I got ready to run out the flat. Stretched his arms to the ceiling. Then I could see the needle marks on the inside of his elbow, the skin grey-silvery there and the yellow under the skin.

~ The gods are just and of our pleasant vices make instruments to plague us.

Lee would never have said that. Lee would have belted the teeth down my throat.

~ What's that mean?

~ That's Shakespeare. 'King Lear'.

~ How do you know it? Did you read it?

~ Fuck, no.

He was not looking at me. Thinking. His face like stone. I was two when he did the murder. Why did Mam call me the same name as him? Did he ask her to?

Then he seemed to come awake again.

~ There was a con I shared a cell with for a while. A teacher.

~ A *teacher*?

~ Yeh. He used to spout that stuff by the yard.

~ A real teacher? Like in a school?

~ Yeh. He was a fucken maniac, so he was.

~ What was he in for?

~ Killing his wife.

I thought, Miss Glennie. Or Mr. Overson. He was married. She would never ... She gets sad if someone treads on a worm in the playground. Mr. Overson, maybe. He would kill. He's nearly killed me a few times yelling in my ear so hard my brain bursts out the other side nearly.

~ So cons aren't all the same, like Mikey. And Lee.

~ Na. There's police in there. Bank managers. Priests. All bent.

~ Any footballers? He nods, then, Shut it now.

He didn't shout. But I knew to shut it.

I made some tea and it was strong and he drank it and made no sound. All he does is quiet with no sound. That is how you get to be in prison, not to be noticed. It is good I am named for my uncle.

It was the same night. I was asleep, then I heard voices. Mam and Gran, Mam crying and Gran roaring. Uncle Mikey talking quiet, then someone banging on my door.

~ Michael, it's me, Mammy.

~ What is it?

~ Open the door to me.

I got out of bed and went to the door and Mam's face was all wet and her arms pulled me, pulled me out. She was holding me and leaning and her belly pushed hard against me and I felt the baby kick.

~ Mam, I can't move, let me go—

~ It's Kevin. He's in hospital. We have to go to him, me and your Gran. We only came home to get money for a taxi off your Uncle.

~ In hospital?

~ He was set on by some lads. Eight of them bastards onto one.

~ Is he bad?

~ Yes, son. Very bad.

Then she put her arms round me again but not for me,

72

for her to cry and I could feel the crying, shaking all her body; then she pushed me away.

~ You'll be all right, so? She brushed my hair back with her hand and her hand was wet with the tears off her cheek.

~ Are you coming back tonight?

~ I don't know . . .

~ Can I come with you?

~ No, son. He's hurt bad. Real bad.

Then she whispered, Pray for your brother.

And she was gone. I watched out the window when the taxi came and her and Gran got in and the taxi moved off, slow like in a dream. I put my face against the glass and the lights of the taxi got small and everything was the same in the street as it was before.

I lay in the bed on Kevo's side and in my head was millions of pictures of Kevo laughing, singing the Christmas songs, having a can or two. Giving me the watch in this room. Kevo reading his comics and sometimes letting me take the ones he's finished. And in a hospital with his eyes shut and a white sheet pulled up to his neck and Mam sitting by, crying and holding his hand and the baby kicking. And when I went asleep after a long time, the dream came again.

The fish was in my hand and its blue eyes were opening and shutting and the mouth was moving.

~ Don't.

In the dream I said nothing, but the fish voice said it over and over, Don't.

Then I was walking along a passage and the walls were white and glassy, like maybe a hospital and the fish was jumping in my hands and screaming, *Don't Micka don't.*

At the end of the white passage there was the bucket. And in the bucket there was something that looked like water. But it was the wrong colour for water. And the fish looked at me and I held it over the bucket and its eyes saw the stuff in the bucket, the water stuff that was pink. Not red but soft, soft pink like a baby's fingers.

I woke up sweating. It was night time still, dark. The eyes of the fish with the eyelashes batting were floating at me in the dark of the room and I went to the window. There was no one there and the street light made the street look green and I didn't know where to go.

Micka was not at school and Glennie said his brother was dangerously ill in hospital. But she would not let us ask any questions. I wonder if Micka is always an unlucky kind of a person and if his bad luck could somehow rub off on me if I go on being his friend? But he does have an exciting life in lots of ways. His family always seems to be in trouble with the police. It was his brother called Kevo who got beaten up and is in intensive care and his other brother

Lee was in prison. When he tells me stuff about them it is almost as interesting as a story in a comic. I bet in his family they are always socking each other on the jaw and seeing stars. He says he has never seen stars. I want to know more about what crimes Lee did, and maybe I could even go to the hospital and see Kevo. I have never seen anyone who has been beaten up. I may even arrive just as he is dying. I am sure I could handle it. I bet Micka will take me if I ask him. I can usually get him to do whatever I want. He likes burgers. And he is good fun to fight with. He knows some sneaky tricks but I am the strongest one and I always win. The last time we were fighting it was because he would not help me with finding the pointing bone.

Bone. A good word, nothing to spare on it. When I write it down, it makes me think of a skeleton. The more I think about the pointing bone the more I want it. But the trouble is, even getting hold of it is the first part of the test. The magic of it will not work unless I can get past the first part. The first part is, I am not allowed to find a thing that is dead already and take a bone from it. I have to kill the thing first.

Micka was offered the choice to be part of the bone magic and he said no. He had no idea what he was turning down, what the power of the bone could have done for us both. So from now on it is just the bone and me. I will have the power of the bone totally for myself, and I will get it without him. Once I have the bone, if he wanted someone done away with sincerely, I could do that for him and he would not even know how. Then he would be sorry he did not choose to be in it from the beginning. Every death will add to its power. And mine.

In 'The Sword and the Stone', the witch Morgan le Fay gets the bone she wants to make her invisible from a cat. She boils it alive. There are plenty of cats around here but I don't see how I could do that. To get a cat in a safe place away from other people, I would need help. And then the boiling part. If you live in a house, not a castle with turrets, the boiling would be a problem.

I have been studying this particular duck in the park and I think it is the right one. It looks at me like it knows what it is for. So maybe it will have to be a duck.

I wish Micka would come back to school. I want to know if his brother is still alive.

Next day I woke up and went in the kitchen. No Mam, no Gran. Uncle Mikey was standing by the cooker, stirring something in a pan.

~ Made your breakfast.

He got the plate and put toast on it and put the bake beans on the toast. It was a good breakfast. He did not eat with me.

~ Do you drink tea at all?

He gave me some tea with sugar and milk. It was good, so hot it burnt my mouth.

~ Is Kevo dead?

~ No. Your Mam and your Gran stayed with him most of the night. They're home now.

~ Can I see Mam?

~ She's sleeping.

~ Is he going to be okay?

~ Come on, you'll be late for school.

Mikey put on his coat and he looked for mine.

~ Do you not have a coat?

~ No.

~ A jacket, even?

~ I lost it. Uncle Mikey, are you going out?

He looked at me.

~ I'm walking you to school.

He held out his hand like I was a babby.

~ I go on my own.

~ Yeh, down the arcade, that's where you go. Or go see the knackers. I'm taking you to school.

We walked to school. It was different. Uncle Mikey talked. Asked me, How are you getting on with your brothers?

~ Okay.

~ They had a tough time over here with your Da. You missed out on it, back home with your Mam.

77

Rathsallagh estate. Me and Mam. Windows with metal cages on. Phone cut off and letters from England she took to her friend to read. And the nights she tried to get me drinking the whiskey with her, crying talking and singing. Ireland. We were there five years.

~ Are you still doing the drawings? That's a good thing. Will you make me a drawing one of these days?

~ Uncle Mikey, why did Mam come back here? Where is Daddy?

He stopped for a breath, looking away and up in the sky so hard I followed his look. In the sun his hair silver as a bullet.

~ Did they not tell you?

~ You tell me.

~ He's dead.

He walked on and the day was the same but I was caught, stopped like a heart with a knife in it.

~ How?

Still walking on; was he angry with me or what?

~ An accident. Ask Maureen. Now is not the time – this is your school, go in now or you'll be late.

We were at the gate. Uncle Mikey stood like a dad, folded his arms and stood right by the wall and watched me in. There were other Mams and Dads there and they saw him watching me. He looked small by them. Lifted his good hand and give me a wave goodbye. I waved. Like the other kids. I wondered did Laurie see.

~ Did you see my Uncle Mikey?

~ No.

~ He came to school with me.

~ Does he have a gun?

~ No.

~ Or a knife?

~ No. He has a big scar on his face.

~ I bet he does have a gun. He wouldn't tell you because you can't keep your mouth shut.

~ Fuck off. My Uncle Mikey is scared of no one. He doesn't need a gun.

~ He's not very clever, though, is he? He got caught, didn't he?

~ You wouldn't say that to his face.

~ I would.

~ You fucken wouldn't.

Miss Glennie sees me kick Laurie under the table and she moves us apart and he makes faces at me until I wish I had a gun.

After another day, Kevo was still bad. Mam went to the hospital but it was hard for her. They did not catch the lads that beat him up so she was scared to be out. I asked could I see him and she always said maybe next week. He is on a breathing machine.

So I went to see him. Never told Mam or Gran. I took a pile of his comics. He has read them all, but there was nothing else.

His ward was called Stevenson. I knew from Gran and Mam's talk. It was easy to find, arrows pointing upstairs and along and I went the way they showed. No one saw me. I went to the door of the ward. A fat nurse was standing by one door, her arms pushed out, resting on her waist like she was there to stop anyone getting past. By another door was two police sitting. That was Kevo's door.

I waited behind a trolley with dirty sheets in until Fat Nurse went into another room. Then I came out. The police was dozy.

~ Hallo, where did you spring from?

~ Can I see my brother?

~ He's not allowed visitors.

~ Only for a minute. I got these for him.

~ No, son. He can't read those, he's too sick.

~ I won't make trouble. I only want to give him these. I won't talk to him or nothing. I'll come straight out.

The police looked at each other. One said, Give this lot an inch . . .

The other one opened the door and looked away down the passage.

~ We haven't seen you, okay. Two minutes. Don't touch anything for Christ's sake.

I went in. Kevo in the bed. Lying straight and stiff, with his arms blue and stuck stiff outside the covers. All laid out dead straight, and tubes with red stuff and yellow stuff going in his arms and up his nose and everywhere. Eyes shut. Not how he sleeps at home, bunched up with his feet kicking me and always pulling the covers off me.

The first bit of his face I could see was a sick white, like white with blue mixed in, but flesh colour too. I walked round the bed. The other side was bad. Mashed up like burger meat with pepper on. It was brown and red and even where his eye should be there was no proper shape, just burger meat. Not even a bandage on. Whoever it was done him over good with a bike chain. On his neck I could see the mark of the chain and some black from the oil of it. Like it was printed on the skin of his neck.

I put the comics on the table by his bed. He never moved. Then I started hearing the noise that was going on there. Noise of an old dog asleep by the fire that doesn't have long to live. There was a grunting in it and a whistle in it. Then I knew what it was. Kevo breathing.

His chest was bare with wires sticking out of it. Somewhere his heart would be, where they had done their kicking, it was blue, nearly black. Eight onto one, all their feet kicking into his chest.

The noise was the worst thing, worse than all the things you could see. Worse than even the mashed-up side of his face. While I was looking at him the noise stopped. Kevo wasn't breathing any more.

I ran out the room and told the police. One of them called a nurse, and she came running, not the fat one but a blonde-haired one that smelled clean, like Miss Glennie. She went in.

~ You better get lost now.

The police pushed me away but I wouldn't go.

~ Is he dead?

~ If he is, he's better off, the other one said. He was not the mean one.

The nurse came out. Looked at me real hard.

~ Did you touch anything?

~ Honest to God, nothing. Is he dead?

She did not look at me any more, just at the police, saying something that Kevo was on a life support and stuff, but not to me, only for them. The door shut. The police sat down like I was not there any more. Nurse put her hand on my shoulder and moved away with me.

~ He's your brother, isn't he? I can see you have the same colour hair. You must be feeling worried about him. Would you like some tea and a biscuit?

She was not throwing me out, then. I said yes. I stood at the door of her kitchen and she switched on the kettle and put biscuits on a plate. Some were chocolate ones. Nurse went on talking in her voice so soft and with her smile like

Miss Glennie, asking what was my name and how old and did I come from a big family and to take a couple of biscuits and she had the mug all ready for the tea and then Big Fat One comes up roaring.

~ Nurse! What do you think you are doing?

~ This is Kevin Doyle's brother. He's having some tea—

~ You are wanted on the ward, nurse. Get back to your work. I'll deal with this.

Blonde one gave me a look and a sorry smile and went away. Fat Nurse switched off the kettle.

~ Visiting hours are 4.30 to 8pm. Members of the public are not allowed on the ward at any other time. *Any other time. Do you hear me?*

All the time looking at me like I was dirt.

~ The patient in room 12 is in intensive care and is not allowed visitors except his mother or a priest. I don't want to see you or any of your family here again or the police will be informed and—

Before she even finished with her shite I was away. I shoved some biscuits in my gob before she could stop me and ran. Fat cow slag bitch cunt. Wouldn't let me have my tea, even. I went in the first lift I could find and the smell in it was like after you've got sick and tried to clean it up but there is still some left. Smelling that and when I closed my eyes seeing Kevo's brown and red burger stuff where his face used to be made me get sick, but I waited until the lift stopped and I got out anywhere. I didn't know if I was near the street or what. There was no toilet or nothing and no people. Only a big pot with an old plant in. I was sick behind it and I couldn't stop like. I couldn't help it. Then I felt dizzy and I ran and ran along corridors until I came to stairs and arrows. I wiped my lips as hard as I could but the taste of the lift smell and the sick would not go out my mouth. It went right down my tubes into my guts.

It was cold outside, I only went a few steps out of the hospital and I started to shake. Like someone bigger and stronger was standing behind me shaking my shoulders like they was an old carpet. I sat on a wall. My legs wouldn't work right. Then people started coming and I crawled behind the wall round the back of an alley and waited till the legs worked again.

CHAPTER 4

March

Mam was out. Kevo and me were eating dinner. Since Kevo got out from the hospital he has a quieter life. He likes to have his dinner ready at six. We were having rashers of bacon and fish fingers and chips.

Then Lee was in, crashing through the door, out of breath like he'd been running a long while. And roaring *Fucking bastards, fucking cunts.* Someone had done him over. His jacket was dusty like he had been laid flat on a floor and pulled along by his collar and his lip was cut. Lee walked from side to side in the room, punching the walls like the room was too small, like it was a cage and he the wild animal. I tried to keep small. Kevo ate his dinner. His knife and fork went up and down, up and down and only his hand shook a small bit. My hand would not work to pick up the fork. I ate a chip in my fingers. Lee would be ok if you did not look him in the eye. Kevo did not look him in the eye.

Lee saw what we were at.

~ Where's my fucken dinner then?

There was no dinner for Lee. Kevo got another plate and put some of his chips on.

~ That's not enough.

Kevo put some of my chips on.

~ And the rashers, Lee said. He was looking at me. I gave him my rashers. He took a fish finger and put it on his fork and shook it in my face.

~ Remind you of anything, does it?

We ate. Lee was still mad, every so often he would break out cursing again. Me and Kevo kept quiet. Then Lee started at me. My hair was shite, my face was shite, everything about me was shite.

~ Just looking at your face makes me want to throw up. You should have been a girl. Then you'd have been good for one thing at least ... eh, Kevo, man? Eh?

~ Lay off it, man, said Kevo, but there was no fight in him. He has changed since the accident. Anything for a quiet life.

~ Lay what?

~ Knock it off.

~ Knock him off, you mean.

~ Jesus!

~ Think I wouldn't? Do ye? Do ye?

Lee's big dirty hand on my hair, stroking, then he grabs it and pulls my head back.

Kevo stops eating.

~ For Christ's sake, can we not eat our dinner in peace?

~ Look at the hard man now, says Lee. All the fight knocked out of him by a kid with a bike chain. Kid like our little gob-shite brother here.

I know I should run now. Get out the flat. Get out from Lee's hand and his belt. But I can't. I can't move. The feel of Lee is so strong in the room, like a yellow cloud of wasps buzzing round his head. He knows I can't move.

Is Kevo scared? He doesn't move either.

~ You want to belt someone, belt the fuckers did this to me. He points to his face.

~ Kill all the fuckers out there, kill anyone but leave us alone for Jesus' sake.

Kevo's voice is weak. Not like in the old days. He is angry but he is more shit-scared. I wish Uncle Mikey would walk in right now.

~ Us, did you say? Leave *us* alone? Lee makes a grab for the collar of my shirt and pulls me up to my feet and my knife and fork drops clattering on the floor and Lee takes the plate and throws it across the room and the good dinner hits the wall and some of it sticks there.

~ You going to stop me? he shouts at Kevo. Anyone going to stop me?

~ Kevo! I scream it once, no more time to breathe before Lee's hand comes pressing down on my mouth, pushing the breath down my throat. His fingers pinch my nose. I can't breathe. I'm going to die now. I'm going to die.

~ Haway, man— Kevo stands up and takes one step towards us. Lee lets go my neck with the one hand. The other hand is still pressing my face, holding me against Lee and I feel the animal inside his chest burning, burning. Lee's knife leaps into his free hand, the blade shoots out faster than you can think. It is pointed at Kevo. Kevo backs off.

~ Don't hurt him. He's our fucking brother.

~ Christ, what they do to you in that hospital? This is a family not a bleeding heart charity. You're gone soft, Kevo. Softer than the shite I'm going to fuck out of his bleeding little arse.

Lee takes his hand off my mouth and the breath swoops into my chest and I cough and Lee shakes me to stop the coughing.

~ This one should never have been born. He's fit for nothing. He's shite.

I look to Kevo. He gave me a birthday card. He said I was his brother.

Kevo steps back to the table.

He sits down real slow.

He keeps his face down. His eyes are into his plate. The good dinner is cold now. He picks up his fork and his knife and he looks into his plate. Up and down. Up and down. I hear the sound of the fork and knife scraping on the plate. The other sound is Lee breathing fast. He laughs. He throws the knife in the table right by Kevo's hand and he laughs and he holds my neck with one hand.

~ Don't hurt him, says Kevo with his mouth full. Like a prayer but with a whispering dull voice. Something is going out of me, like a river of cold black blood through the bottom of my feet. I could fall asleep now, standing up, even.

Lee puts his arm round my waist and lifts me into his room. He can pick me up easy. I am not heavy like Laurie. He drops me on his bed. I am lying across the bed. Lee kicks the door shut with his foot.

I smell Lee's smell on the sheets and the old butts in the ashtray on the floor by Lee's pillow. And I see Lee's calendar with the women in black shiny clothes that leave gaps for their tits and their arses, big as balloons. There was a group, three women, bending over all different ways, with their legs spread wide. One had a whip. She was looking back over her shoulder, smiling at me. She knew what was coming.

~ Get these off. Lee pulls at my jeans. Like in a dream I know what this is. We had films at school. Miss Glennie talked to us. Miss Glennie smiling at us, sitting on her chair and her dress all pink and clean and she telling us how we must say to our parents if anyone . . .

~ Fucking stop that fucking snivelling. You asked for this. I'm going to fuck the arse out of you, and I'll do it until I want to stop.

I shut my eyes.

Lee's hand is tearing my pants. I shove my face down in the sheets that smell of Lee and I hear Lee getting himself ready. He is kneeling with his legs either side of me. A zip undone. Lee breathing like he is in a race. His animal breath on my neck. His hands on the insides of my legs, pulling them open how he wants them. Then the weight of him on me. I try and go away but I can't. Everything around me is Lee. The smell, the sound, the feel of his legs, the colour in my head, Lee's colour, yellow with red worms wriggling in it.

He pushes it inside me.

This isn't the worst thing. The worst thing is Kevo has turned on the radio in the kitchen and he is eating his good dinner. All the time Lee is doing it to me Kevo's knife and fork is going up and down, up and down and the music is going up and down real loud.

Then he pulls it out, and it hurts more than going in.

~ Now get out.

He didn't give me time to put my jeans on, shoved me out the door and kicked it closed. It was hard walking to my bedroom. I sat on the bed. I didn't know where to go now. I was bleeding on the bed and my arse was screaming sore, but I wanted to shit. But if I did, it would hurt worse.

I screwed myself up on the bed as small as I could. And put a big lump of soft covers between my legs and let the shit come out. It hurt but not as bad as I thought it would.

I heard Lee go into the kitchen. They were talking. I heard

the knives and forks. Lee was eating, Kevo watching him. I heard Lee laugh. After a while Kevo laughed. Both of them the same bastards.

Then Lee went out. Kevo came and took the sheets off the bed and threw them out by the bins. There was no clean sheets so I got in Mam's bed. Kevo brought me a mug of tea with sugar but there was no milk.

~ You'll be okay. Put it out of your head. Forget it happened. At least you're not dead, hey? Don't look at me like that.

He shoved a bit of paper in my hand.

~ For your teacher. You can go out with your class. I put Mam's name on. It'll fool them.

He patted my shoulder like I was an old man.

~ You know Lee. Keep out of his way. You'll be okay.

He went out. Mam's bed smelt good. I tried to sleep but it would not come. When I closed my eyes I saw a red diamond. It is like the diamond that has come in my belly. The edges of it are hard and the redness is hard. I know real diamonds aren't red, we have learned that at school, but mine is red and it is hot too. And this diamond will stay with me, so I will never forget what things Lee has done to me. I will feel its cutting edges sometimes when I breathe, I will taste its hotness and redness when things are wrong. And this diamond is there for me only. Not Laurie, not Miss Glennie, not Mam, not even Uncle Mikey. For me.

Next day was the ballet. In the minibus, shouting, pushing, belting heads, trying to get the best seat along the back – like nothing was changed. Miss Glennie counting our heads, smiling at me, takes the note and nods, like, this one is for you, Michael. Down my crack something else for me, hurts when I move too quick.

Laurie didn't come. Then when the bus was ready to go, the engine running and all, his Mam came, talking to Miss Glennie and the driver about why they were late. Laurie sat in the front. He didn't look for me.

I looked out the window, the lights blurred on my eyes, yellow lights in the morning. Yellow is Lee's colour all right; yellow eyeballs, yellow fingers, yellow the skin on his prick.

What about the AIDS? What if he does it to me again? I'll kill him. I'll fucking get Laurie to fucking kill him. Steal something real good and pay Laurie to do it with his bone. Watch Lee die. Ask Laurie if he can do it like that with me watching him die.

No. Not die. Be in agony for the rest of his life. Lee is not tough; he squeals when he gets hurt. The boiling water from the kettle I saw him spill on his leg once when he was drunk, and he squealed like a pup. I could have laughed but he would have thrown the water on me too. I watched and kept small. He tore off his jeans and howled like a wolf over his leg. It was red all right. He shouted at me that he had some pills in his room, to get the fucking pills, but I kept still. He went flapping to his room, one leg of the jeans wet and ripped, dragging along the floor. Lee got the pills and tipped them in his hand and into his mouth all in one, swallowing with his big throat. Grabbing a can from the fridge, drinking, any old can, the lager spilling from his lips down his chest, and he was grunting, falling on the bed. Moaning. I watched and I liked it.

Suppose he drags me in his room again? Tell Mam? What can she do? Miss Glennie? Miss Glennie in our flat, seeing our flat, talking to Lee, talking to Mam, talking to Kevo . . . She is not in our world. Even Laurie is not in our world. Uncle Mikey? Even if I think of telling him I know I can't say it to him. Lee is family. Uncle Mikey is sick and dying. Lee is alive and bad and strong.

We get to the theatre where the ballet is on. Outside the whole wall is lit up like a Christmas tree. Inside, it is like a big room and all huge people wearing big coats and shouting, shouting and pushing. I am scared. Miss Glennie says, You must all keep together. We try and we are pushed away and away and I grab her coat and hold on to the back. She is not looking at me, she is looking at a list and her tickets in her hand and she is not smiling. All the people here are loud. Their faces push into the air, the rich smell of the lipstick off the faces of the women shouts into the faces of the men. All smooth faces and big mouths and eyes like they are in a film and I am watching. The lights are dead bright, lights everywhere hanging like diamonds in big clusters from the ceilings and they are as loud as the shouting.

I touch a fur coat, it is black fur, soft to my hand, and I feel a big animal wriggle under the fur. It is a woman's bum! And she never felt me touch her. She is holding a little drink glass up high and laughing with another woman and her face is the colour orange. I look and look and she never sees me. Her face orange with the orange makeup and her eyes with green on the lids and her lipstick has come off on the glass in the shape of a kiss. No one is laughing at how she looks. Her hair is brushed on the top of her head like candy floss and her teeth show some orange stuck on when she smiles too wide. Then I see Miss Glennie go in and all the class and I push and push to get with them and I get through.

We sit in seats of red velvet. All around is deep, deep red. I close my eyes and see the same red. It is like sitting inside my head. The air is red, the curtains are red. Slowly, slowly they open to the sides and music starts. In front of me is a big head. I can't see. I stand up.

~ Sit down! voices behind me.

~ Haway, I cannat see!

~ Michael, change places with me.

Miss Glennie comes. Smooths her coat, sits down. I have her seat.

*

94

In the next seat to me is a girl called Polly, who is quite a posh girl. She is only in our school because her mother is a teacher in another class. Her mother is not here today. I bet she takes Polly to the theatre a lot though. Probably she has even been to this theatre before, which is why she is not looking at the ballet very much. I know she is looking at me while I pretend to look at the stupid ballet. I wonder if she is thinking about me kissing her.

I keep looking at the ballet and I slide my hand across to her lap and stop. She does not move. Maybe she does not notice. I slide my hand up to her hand, which is in her lap. This time she does notice because she smiles. She keeps her head straight ahead, but she is smiling in a secret way because she thinks she knows what is going to happen. How can she know? I don't even know myself.

I hold her fingers. They are warmer than mine. Softer. She has a ring on her middle finger. There is a school rule that you are not allowed to wear jewellery, but this girl Polly doesn't take any notice of rules. She has gold earrings as well.

I begin twisting the ring round and round on her finger. She shakes her hair back from her eyes and smiles into nothing. There is some music playing, little trickling music that seems to know what I am doing. I stop twisting the ring and pinch her finger against the ring but quite gently. I like doing this. I am watching the dancers and the trick is to look as if no part of you is moving at all; it is just dark enough to seem that we are not even touching, but everything we are saying is done by touch.

Now I am pinching harder. She moves a bit in her seat, but she does not try to take her hand away. I put my thumbnail on the inside of her finger and I press, first gently, then so slowly pressing harder, until I am pressing as hard as I can. What is strange is that she does not cry or take her hand away or try and stop me. When I can't press any harder, I take my thumbnail away and I can feel a big crease in her finger where it went right in.

The next moment she looks at me.

~ Didn't hurt at all. For me to hear, she puts her mouth close to my ear and her warm whisper makes me shiver.

~ Now you do it to me.

~ No.

~ Why not?

~ Why should I?

~ Ssh, goes stupid Miss Glennie.

I want her to do the same to me. But she is still looking at the ballet, leaving her hand in her lap with the fingers open. I slide my hand over to her hand again and this time I pick it up. She puts her eyebrows up. She is surprised.

This time I put her fingers in my mouth. Just the tips. She is wriggling in her chair. Maybe it tickles. She is trying not to laugh. She puts her other hand over her mouth.

I have not thought what I am going to do next, but it happens. Slowly, dead slowly, I start to bite her fingers. I bite down and I bite down and down and down until I start to feel strange. Biting is making me feel excited. That feeling makes me bite more; I can't stop and I don't want to stop.

Now it hurts her. She pulls her hand away from my mouth. She looks at me and she licks her lips with her tongue and puts her head on one side and I don't think she is going to tell. Anyway I don't care. I want to bite again. I take hold of her hand and she wrestles it back. We are not making any noise. Why doesn't she tell on me?

~ Let go, she whispers, and she makes her hand all stiff and bunched up.

~ Only if you do it to me.

~ I don't want to.

~ Then I'll do it to you again.

~ Not so hard.

~ Okay.

She believes me! Her hand goes soft again, and it is still warm, and trembling a little bit. I won't bite the same fingers, I'll go very slowly and carefully.

This time I know what I will feel. Going slowly feels even better. I know when the feeling is coming. The pleasure is to be hurting her slowly and slowly, my body going hard and stiff with the screwing up of all my muscles, biting down, down, down . . .

~ Ow!

In the quiet dark of the theatre, Polly's voice makes everyone jump. Miss Glennie comes along the row behind us and she quickly grabs my collar and Polly's dress.

~ Out. Come outside.

We are in the daylight and the spell is broken. I can see the red marks of my teeth on Polly's fingers.

~ What was all that about?

I wait for Polly to tell. And for the punishment from Miss Glennie. But Polly does not tell.

~ I caught my fingers in the chair. It must be broken.

Miss Glennie looks at Polly's fingers.

~ Is that what happened, Laurie?

~ Yes. It's true, Miss.

We go back in the theatre but this time I am not allowed to sit next to Polly. Miss Glennie sits with her. I am put next to Micka. His nose is dripping and he wipes it on his sleeve. I shut my eyes and think about biting. And girls. This has been an important discovery.

The story was about a boy that was a Prince but the best bit was all the colours of the clothes and the shapes they made when all the dancers moved together. One time there was a row of little girl dancers, only children, Miss Glennie says, called ballerinas. Dresses they had that were the colour of a small rose opening to the sun, moving and shining so soft and sweet, to a circle, to a square, to a line and back again, and all the time their colours stayed like baby roses and their skirts stuck out straight around them, just touched the next skirt and when the lights changed from pink to blue, like magic their clothes all went to purple. That was the best part. The rest of it was long words and the bits with only two people dancing was like grownups talking when they think you are not there and they don't care if you hear or you don't, but the shapes and the colours and all the lights, that was real brilliant and when we went back on the bus I shut my eyes and saw the colours come in my head, all moving to the music and that was my day and it was the best of my day.

In the bus I remembered Uncle Mikey sick like the Prince. If he was not sick he could maybe stay with us again and send Lee packing. Mikey makes a good breakfast and stays with me while I eat. I will ask Laurie if he has got the bone yet with the magic in that kills. Maybe he could give Lee the AIDS from Mikey. Mikey has gone away to Ireland. Kevo told me. Gran went too. They went when I was at school and no one said, so in the morning they were there and when I came home they were gone. Gran's blue coat was gone and her nighty from Mam's bed. There was nothing of Mikey's things because he only had one bag coming from the prison.

That night Mam and Kevo sat up and played cards and

they would not talk about Gran or Mikey. Kevo is not sleeping in our bed, so maybe Lee has gone away again. I lay in the bed that night with the light on and no sheets. Life made me cold and the bed was hard and the dream was there like a fox, waiting and waiting on me falling to sleep.

The day after our class went to the ballet I broke my arm. It was because of my mother.

We were walking in Eldon Park in the freezing cold. My mother has this idea that if all human beings spent seventy-five per cent of their lives in the open air they would not grow old so quickly because their cells would stay full of oxygen. And she thinks the best oxygen is in the air around trees. When we are in the park, she breathes a lot and does some exercises and sometimes I climb trees while I am waiting.

We stopped by a massive tree I had not seen before. There was a branch above my head. If I could have reached that branch to start off, I could easily have climbed the whole tree. But it was too high and there was nothing up to that branch, no knobs or splits in the trunk, and it had the kind of smooth bark that has no ridges.

There was no one else around. My mother stopped her deep breathing and looked at the tree for quite a while. She looked up through the branches and she was smiling to herself. Then she stroked the bark and put her ear to the trunk and listened. Then she held out her hand to me.

~ Laurie, wouldn't you like to climb this beautiful beast?

I came up close to the tree and I saw why she stroked the bark and scraped her long nails along it. Underneath the smooth bark, its muscles rippled like the flesh of a giant lizard walking slowly.

~ I can't. I can't reach up to that branch.

~ But if you could, it would be easy after that, wouldn't it?

~ Suppose so.

I wished some other people would come. My mother leaned against the tree with her eyes screwed up as if there was cigarette smoke in the air and she looked at me, smiling at her thoughts.

~ You're not scared, are you, baby?

I hate being called baby. I said I wasn't scared.

She held out her arms to me.

~ I'll lift you up. Don't look at me like that; you look just like your father. Do you think I can't lift you?

She put her arms around my knees and lifted me up. Her body was as tight as a wire. She went on lifting me until I could touch the branch. But it wasn't high enough to get my arm over it. She let me down. I thought her idea was finished.

~ We'll go again. I need to lift you from lower down.

Before I could say anything, her arms were gripping like metal rods into my legs, nearly down by my ankles. She gritted her teeth and breathed in and lifted me up. This time I could get my arms around the branch.

~ Quick, pull yourself up onto the branch! she shouted, and it was good that I did because she let go at once and started laughing.

~ Go on, my Tarzan, climb higher! I told you I could lift you.

The branch was a perfect thickness, and it had knobs on that my hands found easily and soon I was sitting on the branch swinging my legs way above her head.

~ Oh, how I would love to be up there with you! Stand up, Laurie. See how high you can climb now.

She is watching me as I climb up and up. It is easy in one way, but not if you think about how you will get down. Every time I want to stop, she says to go higher.

~ Don't think. Just do it. You can do it.

And she is pressing herself against the trunk of the tree, stretching her arms wide around it, but it is too big for her arms to meet.

So I go as high as I want, well, maybe higher than I want because something in my mother's face is making me. She thinks I am soft and too scared to go higher. But in the end I have to stop because I slip and nearly fall and it makes my heart bang so hard I can't concentrate any more. So I start to come down and this is not easy at all because she starts telling me where to step and when I do there is no branch there or it is too far away to reach and it reminds me of when we all used to be in our car with my father driving and my mother making suggestions about over-taking and my father getting irritated and saying, If I had done that, Josie, we would all be dead by now.

But at last I get back to the big branch and it is too far to jump to the ground. My mother stands underneath. She smiles and stretches up her arms and her coat swings open. She looks so beautiful you cannot believe that she could do anything bad.

~ What shall I do now?

~ Can't you jump from there?

~ You know I can't.

~ Work something out, she says teasing me, and I hate her.

~ *You* work something out. This was your idea.

~ But you wanted to do it, didn't you, baby?

~ Just get me down, you – you cow.

I did not mean to say that but I could see the keeper coming and I was cold and she had teased me enough.

~ Jump. I'll catch you. You know I can. You know how strong I am. Jump.

This was not a good idea and I knew it but the keeper

was getting closer and I remembered her lifting me with her body as strong and stiff as a wire, so I jumped.

I heard her laugh. I must have closed my eyes. I hit the ground. She was not there.

~ See? I knew you could do it.

She had moved. She said she would catch me.

I got up and there was a strange new pain in my arm and everything swam around and went black.

The day after the ballet I was home on my own. I was making a drawing. The bell rang. I did not go.

A voice shouted through the letterbox: Let me in, it's Sandra.

I opened the door. It was a woman standing there with a little kid in a buggy.

~ Hello, Micka, she says.

I never seen her before.

~ I'm your Auntie Sandra.

~ What Auntie Sandra?

~ This here's your little niece Donna. Say hello to your Uncle Micka, sweetheart.

Auntie Sandra comes in the kitchen.

~ No one else in? Aren't you going to make me a brew?

She starts to make a cup of tea. She parks Donna in the buggy. Donna stares around the flat. She has big eyes, blue.

Her hair is blondy and in curls with a velvet pink ribbon. Not the same colour as our hair.

~ So where's your Mam?

~ Out.

~ Lee here?

~ No.

~ Know where he is?

~ No.

~ Don't talk much, do you?

Donna starts roaring. Straight away Sandra picks her out the buggy and cuddles her. Kisses her cheeks and nose. Smooths her hair. Doesn't put her back in the buggy. Walks around the kitchen like it was hers, opening the drawers, poking things.

~ This baby has everything, she's perfect. You can tell him that from me.

She sticks her chin out like I was arguing with her. Gets a biscuit from her bag and gives it to Donna. Donna stops crying, stares at the biscuit with tears standing in her eyes; they look bigger and bluer with the tears standing in them. Sandra takes a blondy curl in her finger and strokes along it.

~ I don't need him, you tell him. We don't need anything from him.

~ Tell who?

~ Your shagging brother, who d'ye think? This is his.

~ Lee? That's Lee's baby?

She pours out the tea and pushes the biscuits across to me.

~ Want some? Help yourself. Why aren't you at school? Are you wagging?

~ It's Saturday.

Auntie Sandra giggles. She puts too much milk in my tea. Bends her head over the baby so I see the roots of her hair, dark brown. The rest is blondy like Donna's hair, fluffed out on her shoulders. She is wearing a green dress, tight, shorter than her knees. I can see the shape of her at the top of her legs. Mermaid dress, so tight I wonder can she walk at all.

Donna has some tea and milk in her bottle and she sits quiet in the buggy. Auntie Sandra cleans her face with a little paper flannel thing. Then she kicks her shoes off and crosses her legs. Up the space in her dress I can see green darkness.

~ What you staring at? You're all sex maniacs in your family, do you know that? Well, I'm not ashamed of my body. I'm not a Catholic and I don't believe in sin. You can tell Lee that from me.

~ Are you married to Lee?

~ What do you think? Think I'd marry a bastard like Lee and get the living daylights belted out of me for the rest of my life? No chance. What, wake up with that on the pillow beside me for the next fifty years? No thanks.

Lee's bed and the smell and the butts and the women on his wall looking over their shoulders . . .

~ Watch it, you nearly spilt your tea, Micka. You all right? Have another biscuit. You're hungry, aren't you?

~ Mam will get home soon.

~ Well, when she does, you can tell her what I told you – oh, yes, and tell Lee that we're going to Liverpool to live with my sister. She's got two kids, see, and I'm going to stay home and mind them while she works. I love kids. I know how to bring up a kid; you tell Lee that. This baby is going to have *everything*, and he's never going to see her again. Tell him. Tell him to get a fucking life – haway, are you doing a picture of me?

I push the drawing across the table and watch to see what she does. She stops talking. She stops smiling. She stares at the drawing.

~ Jesus Christ!

The drawing is Lee. He is having his prick eaten by wild animals. His hands are pulled up over his head and nailed to a wall like Jesus on the cross. Auntie Sandra looks at me with a sorry face, like I have hurt her baby. She pushes the picture back to me.

~ And you, you get out of here as soon as you can. You're not bad like the others, but you don't stand a chance in this place.

I get up. I want to go away. But she has a loud voice and it pins me, standing by the table.

~ The thing is, your Mam can't cope. She's not a good

Mam, she's not looking after you like she should. I mean, this place is a tip. You get out as soon as you can.

Auntie Sandra covers Donna up with a fluffy blanket.

~ We're going to the park now. Feed the ducks. Donna loves feeding the ducks, don't you, darlin'?

She kisses the baby. Then she stands straight and comes towards me and puts her arms round me and kisses me and I smell roses off her.

~ You poor little lad. Take care, Micka.

She lets herself out. Her high heels go clatter clatter down the passage. She can walk away from our world. She can walk away from Lee. She's left her biscuits and the paper towel with her smell on it, and her brassy voice is clashing in my head till I want to break something, break her, break it all up.

I tear up the drawing. I eat the biscuits and watch telly till everything in my head goes quiet.

At the hospital, we said it was an accident. My mother seemed quite like other mothers while we were talking to the doctor and getting the plaster put on. She said things like, I worry so much when he climbs trees. If only I had been there in time to stop him, this would never have happened.

She made it all sound true and real and I believed it

myself while we were in the hospital. It was a kind of game for us both to fool everyone.

It is strange how she can become so many people. I never know for sure what she will say or do. There is a word for this; *unpredictable.*

When my parents lived together it was a word they used a lot. My father said my mother was unpredictable. She thought that was good. She said he was too predictable. She threw the word at him like a hedgehog whenever she was angry with him.

I can see that being unpredictable can be quite dangerous and stop you even from saving your child if it jumped off a branch and you didn't feel like catching it. But then, as she said when we were going home in a taxi, life would never be exciting if it wasn't dangerous. And I suppose she is right.

When Mam came in, I told her about Auntie Sandra coming here. She said I was not to say Auntie Sandra. She is a slag and a tart and she took Lee's giro.

We ate some sausages. My Gran cooks a good thing with sausages; it has a kind of pancake mixed in it and keeps you from getting hungry so quick. It is called Toad in the Hole. Mam does not do it because it uses up the oven. Before Gran went away, she said she would teach me some cooking. But I would not do it if Lee was around.

If Gran was still here she would help with the baby. I wonder will she come back or did Mam send her away for good? And was there a row or did Gran have to go with Uncle Mikey? Maybe Gran will come back. Mam won't say.

My Mam has grey hair. One time she dyed a different colour into it and Lee said it was like a Brillo pad gone rusty. My Mam has a tired face with no cheeks. She does not have tight dresses like Sandra. That is how a mam should look. Not like a mermaid with high heels.

I had a dream about the new baby. It was like Donna with angel hair and a little blue dress. In my dream the baby got out the buggy in the kitchen and came walking to me, holding her hands out to me, smiling. She put her mouth to my cheek and I saw her eyes were red where the white part should be and she bit my cheek and spat it out and I was bleeding in the dream, and I pushed her away but she bit the other cheek and her teeth were silver colour like metal and sharp like a saw and the bit of my cheek hung between them and it was the colour of liver.

A letter came for Mam. She does not read so great. It was from Gran and she wanted to know what was in it and only I was home. She opened it up and I saw the stamp was from Ireland. She gave it to me to read to her.

It said, *Dear Maureen and lads, Well, they have let him*

come home at last and here I must stay until he is taken from me. The land is good and the old house is still standing and we are not coming back. And I am sorry with all my heart I will not be there for the baby but you have your lads and they must do their part. Give Micka a kiss for me and tell him I was asking for him. And if he wants to send his Uncle one of his own pictures that would be a kindness to a dying man.

So no more Gran, and Uncle Mikey gone for good. Mam cried, but she cries easy. I never cry.

CHAPTER 5
April

~ Oh God, Michael! Mam shouts.

I am looking out the window at a dog far down on the ground. The dog is lost or mad; it runs in circles.

~ Michael, run quick for the doctor. Mam's voice stops. I go in the kitchen and she is lying on the floor with her coat on and her legs open and she is breathing funny and I see her huge belly moving all by itself.

I look in her purse for money for the phone. She has 37p in. I take the purse and run down the stairs and the first person I see is Miss Inglis with her shopping. She is the witch, but there is no one else. She only has to walk up one lot of stairs to her flat and I go with her, pulling her by the shopping, and she is all the time trying to shake my hands off.

~ It's the baby coming, me Mam is on the ground, you got to help us, please . . .

Miss Inglis has a grey face with a look on her that says, you bother me and I'll see you in your dreams. They say she was a teacher; well I wouldn't have a witch like her for my teacher. I think about running but she puts the key in her front door.

~ You'd better come in.

She pushes me in ahead of her. Puts the shopping down by the phone in the hallway. I lift the phone and she snatches it out of my hand.

~ I'll do it. They won't trust a child's voice.

She calls the ambulance. Puts the phone down and looks at me. Shakes her head.

~ They said twenty minutes, what is the world coming to? You'd better go back and wait with your mother.

~ I can't.

If I went back to our kitchen there would be no one and only me to watch Mam's belly for twenty minutes and her moaning and the belly twisting to one side and the other side. Maybe the baby would come and I would be on my own with it. Miss Inglis reaches out her crabby hand and pushes me along the hall, out.

~ I've done all I can for you, now you have to go. Tell your mother you have head lice.

~ No I never.

~ Your head is alive with them. Tell her.

She slams the door and I give it a good kick. Old fucking witch slag. But I still have the 37p.

I go slowly up the stairs and back to our flat. The door is

wide open. Maybe the ambulance has come. But when I go in, there is no one there except Mam.

I go slowly in the kitchen and Mam is standing by the table and she is leaning on the edge of the table, resting all her weight on one hand and that hand is dead white with the heaviness. She is holding her side with the other hand and breathing slow and hard, like she has to think before she takes a breath.

~ Has the baby stopped coming?

She tries a smile. Her face is not a good colour. Then it screws up and her eyes are tight and she has to walk up and down, one hand all the time pressing into her side. Maybe she is trying to squeeze the baby in.

~ Did you call the ambulance?

~ They said twenty minutes.

~ Sweet Jesus! I can't wait that long.

~ Mam, you have to, there's no one. Don't.

~ Help me get in the bedroom. I need something in there.

I try not to get close to the baby shifting inside her belly but she holds me to her, dead close, leaning on my shoulders with all her weight. We get to the bedroom and she bends over the bed, holding on to me, tries to kneel on the bed but she can't keep still.

~ Mam, is Gran coming back?

~ Get me fags on that table.

I give her the fags and she starts crying.

~ Mam, let go of us, I need to go to the toilet . . .

~ No you don't.

She is gripping my arm tight with the one hand, and her eyes are shut and she holds my hand and squeezes so hard it is purple, and she moans and moans. Then she slowly lets go. She has dropped the fag and I give it back to her. She turns over on the bed and there is wet there. She has wet the bed.

~ Why did Gran go away?

~ Go to the window and see is the ambulance here yet.

I look down. The dog is still there, lying in the road, scratching under its leg.

~ Where's the baby going to sleep? There's no more rooms.

~ Jesus! Mam shouts. I wonder is she roaring at me but it is the same as before, she is moaning again and I keep away.

Then I hear the ambulance coming with its siren going and blue lights flashing and it nearly hits the dog, but the dog runs off and the two of them come round the back of the ambulance and fetch out the stretcher, and I am down those stairs so quick and up the stairs again with them and into the bedroom.

They get her on the stretcher and she shuts her eyes and I am gone out of her head; it is only her now, and the baby that's coming. One of the men says, Who's going to look after you while she's in hospital, bonny lad?

~ My brother. He's gone out to the shops.

~ How old is your brother? Are you sure you'll be okay here on your own?

Mam opens her eyes and says, Michael is a good boy. He won't get into trouble, will you, Michael? He'll be grand with Kevin, won't you?

~ Yes, Mam.

All I want is Mam away to the hospital safe.

~ Good lad, says the ambulance man. I watch from the window while they put Mam in. A few people watching, like it was an accident. The blue flasher light goes on the ambulance, and it goes away.

Kevo didn't come home. I went to the shop and spent the 37p on some crisps and sweets. I tried to watch telly but my eyes kept seeing Mam all squeezed up with her eyes shut and moaning. This is how it is having a baby. Did she do that when I was coming? Did I make her hurt so bad? How is there a hole big enough for a baby to come out?

I watched the telly but it could not shut the noise of Mam moaning out of my head. I went in the bedroom and saw her fags where she dropped them. I thought I would have a fag but there was no matches there. Nor in the kitchen.

I went in Lee's room and the tray was still there with the butts by Lee's bed and the pictures on the wall and the smell of Lee in the room still. I kept the door open. In the room on my back was a hot feeling like some eyes watching me from a cupboard or under the bed. I put my back against the wall and I knocked a pile of Kevo's comics down and they fell this way and that way and I packed them back in the pile but it kept slipping and slipping and Lee's eyes were all over me and in my head he was laughing and taking off the belt with the wolf head. I left the comics and ran out the room and kicked the door shut.

I went to bed in Mam's bed. All the lights were on. It is good the electric has been put back on. Gran has got good ideas; she gets things done.

In the morning Kevo was there. He woke me.

~ You got a new sister, snotface.

~ Is Mam okay? When's she coming home?

~ We'll go and see her later, take some flowers.

~ I'm hungry.

Kevo feels in his pocket, gives me a fiver.

~ Run down the shop and get some bread and sausages and some smokes. And you can have 50p for yourself.

Kevo and me are in the hospital. It is the same one Kevo was in when they beat him up. He hates to be back there. Hates the smell.

We go up to Mam's ward. She is in bed and there is a cot right by her. The babby is red. Her face is squashed looking and her eyes shut. She does not have much hair. It is red, like mine.

~ Did it hurt her, being born?

~ Ah, come here, son.

Mam opens her arms and I climb on the bed and she gives me a kiss. The bed has paper sheets and the pillow has a paper cover. Mam smells of the hospital. There is not much of her today. Her big belly is gone. Her hair is thin and it sticks to her head like she has put grease on it. I go up and down and look at the other babies. They all look different. Some are much bigger, some with more hair, some with a tooth. They are not so red as our baby.

~ Kevo, is she always going to be that red?

~ Yeah, poor little cunt.

Kevo has bought Mam some flowers and fags. The flowers came from the hospital shop and they smell of hospital like everything else there. There is no flower smell off them no matter how hard you sniff.

~ Leave them things alone, what you trying to do, eat them?

~ Kevo, Mam says, make sure Michael gets a good dinner tonight. I'll be home tomorrow; I asked could I come home early.

Kevo is standing up; he has had enough hospital.

~ Okay, okay, yeah, come on, Micka, we have to go.

~ Don't you want to know the baby's name? It's Paula. What do you think? Do you like it?

Kevo is away down the ward. So she has a name. She is in our family now. For ever.

*

There was a meeting last night. My father came right into the house. It was the first time since he left that Josie had allowed him in, and things have changed a lot. He frowned and looked up to the ceiling when he saw the carpets were gone and the newspapers under the table and my school-books not in a neat pile in the bookcase like they used to be when he lived here.

I got as far away from Brian and Josie as I could, so they could not squash me in between them like they did before. They were sitting a long way away from each other and my mother was cutting something up. My father had his work files and his briefcase and he put it on the floor in front of him, resting on his legs like a shield. Then he started.

~ Laurie, if you insist on eating in here, may I suggest that you use a plate?

~ Leave him alone, my mother said.

~ I'm trying to get him to behave like a civilised human being. My father sounded tired, like he had already given up that fight. Not like my mother; she was cutting the material and sometimes she took a piece in her teeth and tore it like a lioness devouring her prey. When she looked at me, her eyes were sparkling. She likes to fight with my father. She knows she will always win.

~ Let's get down to business, he said.

~ What business? I said.

~ Well, Laurie, your mother and I have been discussing the future.

~ What future?

~ Your future.

~ The thing is, we wonder if you are happy at your school, said my mother. She stopped cutting for a minute and stared at me.

~ It's okay. No worse than anywhere else.

~ I *wish* you would get the child a plate, Josie, said my father. She made a little wriggle of her shoulders like I do sometimes.

~ What's going on? I asked.

~ We've found a new school for you.

They said it together, then they looked at me. As if they were a pair of scientists and I was the experiment. I said, No thanks. I don't want to go anywhere else. My school is okay. I won't go anywhere else.

~ But that is exactly the problem – and Brian suddenly started ticking a list of things off on his fingers – you don't go to school at all, you regularly truant, your schoolwork is giving cause for concern, soon there will be some crucial tests coming up and—

~ Fuck this, my mother shouted, and she waved the scissors towards my father, *you* want this, Brian, you, not me. Things are fine as they are. Laurie doesn't want to change,

I don't want to change. It's you, the same as it's always been.

~ Josie, be reasonable—

~ Shut it, Brian! I've had enough!

When she shouts like that her voice is not soft and posh but sounds like the West Country she came from. I saw my father getting irritated, and gripping his briefcase to stop his hand from shaking (or maybe from strangling my mother). He pulled at his tie with his other hand and made a noise in his throat to get her attention.

~ We *will* have this discussion, we *will* get things settled, one way or another, and we will do it tonight because things cannot continue the way they are.

My father said this all in one breath, but she was not bothered. She dropped all the bits of the cut dress on the floor and I suddenly saw it was a special dress he had bought her once when they had a row and made it up. And at the same time he saw it too, and he pressed his lips tight together and looked up at the ceiling and talked to the ceiling.

~ All right. Have it your own way.

~ Let's do what Laurie wants. After all, it's his life.

~ I want things to stay how they are, I said.

~ There, you see? Laurie wants things to stay how they are.

He looked at her like a dog that is waiting to be kicked. Then he waved his finger at me.

~ Laurie, kindly go to your room.

~ No. Stay here, Laurie.

~ Josie—

~ It's his life, Brian. He's very nearly an adult.

~ He's eleven! For God's sake!

~ Are you going to calm down, Brian, because if not you can leave now.

He got up and brushed the dust off his trousers. He came across to where I was sitting and I waited for him to kiss me or pat me on the head. I felt him hovering near me wanting to do something and Josie watching him with a smile on the side of her face. So he carefully picked up some crumbs I had left on the chair and put them in my mother's ashtray. Then he went out. My mother's mouth went all loose and she nodded towards the cupboard.

~ Get the bloody bottle, darling.

I got the bottle. She smiled a lot then and stroked my hair.

~ We've won. You realise what this means? We are strong, my love.

I completely believed her that night, and I remember laughing with her, and how she let me taste her drink. I imagined that she thought I was her equal, almost an adult. I knew she was a bit mad, but I thought that was good, because a truly mad person would be strong, and it was best to have her on my side. I thought I had to choose between being a bit mad myself, or being ordinary and pathetic and a doormat. That is what she called him that night. She did not even waste her energy hating him, she made him seem not important. I would do anything not to have her think I was a doormat.

Kevo was minding the baby while Mam was down the launderette. She woke up and cried for her bottle.

~ Are you going to feed her, Kevo?

~ In a minute. Here. Watch this first.

He got her bottle with the milk in that Mam put in and he tipped it down the sink. He had a fag in his mouth and the ash fell in the sink and the noise it made was like rain falling on the side of old Babs' kettle.

~ Will I fetch her in?

~ Why not?

I went to Mam's room and took her up. She was wet all through. Screaming for her bottle. Kevo had it in his hand. When he sat down I saw what was in the bottle, and it was brown.

~ That's not her milk . . .

~ Bring her over and watch this.

He held the babby close and put the titty to her mouth. She sucked it like she was mad for it. Then she pushed her mouth away and made a face like she was sick. She cried and turned her head away from the titty.

~ What is that stuff?

~ Only a drop of McEwans. She never learns this trick. Watch again.

Kevo started laughing. He held the bottle by her mouth again and she took it and sucked away.

~ See how thick she is? Doesn't have the sense she was born with. Just like her Mammy.

She did the same thing again. Made a face and turned her head away. The beer dripped out her mouth. She started screaming again. Kevo bounced her up and down.

~ Ah, who's a good girl then? You can get her milk now.

I cleaned the bottle and put the milk in. Kevo gave her to me to hold. She was struggling at first like she would not take the titty. Then she took it all right.

~ Did you play that trick on me when I was a babby?

~ Not me. Lee.

She sucked and sucked till her face was all twisty and tired with the crying and sucking. Kevo lit another fag.

~ Do you ever get her to smoke?

~ Don't be putting ideas in my head.

~ Will you change her nappy?

~ I will not. Leave that for Mam; it's her job.

I put the baby in bed. The bed was all wet but she went to sleep all right.

*

In the park all the leaves were coming green, just opening, unfolding. There is a roundy shape tree with pale green leaves and the shape of the leaf is roundy like the tree. You can pull the flesh of the leaf away from the bones and it makes a skeleton leaf. I was doing this and Laurie was digging for worms to give the ducks and he was in a mood.

~ Tell it.

~ I won't.

~ Tell me the dream or I won't ever tell you anything.

~ Haway and fuck yourself with the raggy end of a stick.

He fell over nearly, laughing. He had a tube of Rolos in his pocket and he threw them over to me.

~ Here, have as many as you want.

The dream about the talking fish is not right to tell him. But there is always a dream. Laurie wants to know a dream. So I eat the Rolos and tell him.

~ You know bluebottles? You know that time you showed me how to stick a pin through a bluebottle and pull off the wings and make it into a new insect?

Laurie has found a worm and he throws it in the pond and a duck comes up quick.

~ New species, yeah. So?

~ That's the start of my dream. I have a pin through me, into a block of wood and there is a row of us all pinned to the same . . .

~ Am I in the row? Am I pinned?

125

~ No.

~ Well fuck you, why not?

~ It's a fucken dream, man! You cannat choose people in dreams!

I walk away and Laurie is up after me and throws me down on the grass and puts his knees on my arms.

~ Like this, is it like this, being pinned?

~ Get off me!

~ Tell me the dream, you wanker.

~ We are pinned in a row and I can't move, only my head . . .

~ Does it hurt?

~ No. We can't feel anything. Only we hold our breaths. The other boys in the row make faces at me. And I make faces back.

~ Like how?

~ Like this. Then there is a flip, and the piece of wood goes flying into the water with us on it.

~ What do you mean, a flip? Where does the water come from?

~ I don't fucken know, it's just a dream.

Laurie gets off of me. He talks like Miss Glennie.

~ No need to swear, Michael. Share out the Rolos like a good boy.

That dream was last night, and the colours of it are coming at me strong now. I can't even talk now. If I do, I will cry or

126

get sick or punch out at Laurie. Pinned like a fly with wings torn off. Pinned so we can't get away.

~ I'm sick, me. Sick of it.

~ Sick of what?

~ All of it.

He has got six worms in a bag. There used to be marbles in that bag but he sold them. He looks in at the worms. Looks at me on the grass. He smiles his bad smile. He has let the dream go for a while. He gets something out the bag.

I put a leaf in my mouth. If you chew it, it goes to soap in your mouth. Not the taste, but the slime and bubbles of soap.

Laurie has a big glass thing. He puts a worm under it. He is moving it around.

~ What you doing?

~ See this. It's the power of the sun.

He holds the glass and the sun is there under the glass, down to a point of light. The worm is under the point.

~ Just like under a laser beam. It's frying.

The worm is twisting, rolling, twisting, and he holds the point of the sun on it. I push his hand. He smacks it away.

~ Worms can't actually feel pain. They have no nerves like we do.

~ Then why's it go like that, rolling around?

~ Probably doesn't like the light. They die if they get dried out. If I leave it under the glass like this, in the end it will go on fire.

~ It won't—

~ It will—

~ It never will—

~ Want to see it burst into flames? It's going to die anyway when I give it to the ducks. Its time is up.

He has a dead steady hand. He is quiet. The worm does not matter. It does not feel pain. He lets me hold the glass. The worm does not feel pain.

Then he laughs.

~ It's good fun, isn't it? Having power of life and death.

The pup died but that was not power. I give him the glass back. His mouth is red like a fox.

~ Hey, Micka! Suppose we had power over another human being. Just for a day. An hour, even. Get them on their own. We could try things. Like with this worm.

The worm has stopped still. It never went on fire.

~ Burn them?

~ No, other things. Experiments. Like scientists. Get them somewhere and try things.

~ Get who?

~ Someone small.

And he is right. We could do it. No one telling us. Try things. Do what we like.

He holds the glass over his hand.

~ See how long I can bear it. If I leave it there, it will actually burn.

128

Laurie is mad. He gives me the glass to hold. But while I am thinking do I want to hold it on his hand the sun goes in.

~ So who will we take?

~ You're up for it! Good man, Micka!

~ Who, though?

~ I think ... a girl. Don't you? It has to be a girl.

A girl would not fight. A small girl on her own.

~ A bairn, like? My sister?

~ Has she got teeth?

~ Small, and without her Mam or anyone, and we could bring her here—

~ Yeah, brilliant idea, bring her to the park with millions of people watching. We want to get her on her own.

~ And do what we like—

~ A girl, but she must have teeth—

~ Paula has a tooth.

~ Not her. She's just a baby. We want someone that can walk. And bite. A stray girl.

The red diamond is there today, in the belly. Heavy and hot in the guts. No one to stop us. We could do what we want. Laurie is right. He smiles like a fox and so do I.

We could have some fun with a girl. A stray girl.

The worm is still in the grass. He picks it up and looks.

~ See, there's a sort of a burn mark.

~ Haway. Let it go.

I spit out the leaf and it is a ball of green slime and bubbles. Laurie throws the worm out into the duck pond. He puts his hand in the bag of worms and takes out another. He told me he ate a live worm once. It tasted of earth.

CHAPTER 6

May

It is time now. There are some jobs to be done with the pointing bone and it would be cowardly to put them off any longer. Now my arm is out of plaster I can get through the hole in the fence and back to my old place in the park. I have to get my own pointing bone and it must be from something that I must kill.

My parents have shut up about changing school, so I think the danger has passed. They never ask me if I miss some days. Perhaps they have decided it's easier to let me run my own life like an adult. I am learning about cooking things for myself. The best thing for cooking is a frying pan. You can fry just about anything. And it's quick. Josie never minds what I cook. She never seems hungry. Last night I had fried bread and fried frozen peas and fried chocolate digestives (which were not such a good idea). She is good at not asking questions. This gives me plenty of time alone in my room to plan things. I have decided to go to the park to begin the first stage of the bone magic. The first stage will be quite hard and I suppose even dangerous if I am caught. After that it will all be easy.

I must go alone and as late at night as possible. And of course I am not to speak to anyone else about this. I wonder if even writing about it in my logbook will weaken the magic. But it is important to write down exactly what I am doing because if ever I need to do it again I will have to do it the same way or it won't work.

Tuesday. This is what I did. I went to the park when it was nearly time to close, just about sunset. I went to my old place by the pond – what used to be my place, but some nosy keeper has been in there and taken away the camouflage and wrecked my den. But the hollow space is still there, where you can sit and watch the ducks and no one can see you. The rushes are very tall and the pond is shallow there, so I can put my hand in the water and not even disturb the rushes as much as a whisper of wind.

Now is the time of year when the ducklings have grown a bit and they get adventurous and their mothers are too busy with their heads down in the water to keep an eye on them properly. There is one family I specially noticed; they are just ordinary ducks with no special markings or anything and there are five ducklings in that family. They look surprised when they come out of the water that they have such big feet and they trip over each other a lot. Ducks have got very small brains, I believe.

Anyway, there is one duck that has a pale beak and more black feathers than the others. He is the slowest and he gets left last. He was the one I chose.

I had some bread and I rolled it into pellets and started throwing it towards where they were standing at the edge of the pond. They noticed the bread and they began fighting and pecking; then slowly I started throwing the bread nearer and nearer to where I was sitting and some of them started to come near me. It says in my encyclopaedia not to catch the eye of a wild bird because it will be frightened, so all the time I looked down at the ground and just quickly glanced up from time to time. It was good because the sun had set now and everyone had gone from the park and it was all dead quiet, with just a duck quacking across the pond sometimes, and I felt like another wild animal living there, preying.

The slow duck came nearest to me. I knew he would. It was part of the magic I had done already when I chose him. I reached out my hand and there were a lot of bread pellets there, and I could feel the duck looking at my hand. I glanced quickly at him and his neck was stretched out towards the bread and he was making practice grabs towards it. I moved my hand back a tiny fraction of a centimetre and he did not even notice. He moved closer. His beak touched my hand.

I knew when he pecked the bread that I had to be incredibly patient. It was too soon to grab him. I let him peck and take some bread and walk a little way away. I waited until he came again. This time he did not do the practice pecks; he came close up to me straight away and took the bread. His guard was down. I closed my hand over his beak and with my other hand I got hold of his neck and pulled him to me. All the other ducks made a huge quacking and shot into the water and paddled away as fast as they could.

I stayed dead still, sitting in the hollow in the rushes and I got the duck on my lap into a sort of comfortable position so I could talk to him. It was important that he knew what was going to happen, so that his spirit would join in the magic. This is what I whispered to him.

~ You and I are going to do some magic on living things. Animals and people. We will start off with small animals and move on to humans. You are alive now, but soon you will be dead and in your bones will be a deep wish for revenge. You will bring death to living and healthy animals that I will choose. I will listen to your voice because you will know what it is like to be dead. And you will obey my commands because I have killed you and I am still alive. And together we will kill. Kill. Kill.

I said Kill lots of times because I wanted it to be the last word the duck heard before I killed it, and each time I said it louder.

I put my hands around his neck and started strangling it. It was much harder than I thought it would be. When I told Micka I had cooked ducks before it was not actually a fact. It was an idea that I made into a fact.

The neck of a duck is stronger than you would think and the feathers are very short and smooth there, with lots of oil on, so when they are in the water for hours the duck doesn't get cold. I could not get a good grip on him and my hands got very slippery and sweaty and the rest of the duck was flapping a lot and his feet were quite sharp, and I kept on squeezing and twisting at the same time but it was like squeezing a really strong rope. Then I tried snapping the neck quickly, but whichever way I snapped it, it bent like rubber.

In the end the duck stopped struggling and just in case it was not properly dead I held its head under the water and waited until no more bubbles came up.

I had respect for that duck, because it put up a strong fight for its life. And I think it will be powerful in the magic because of this. Experiments like this should be thought of as scientific research because then you have a reason to go on doing it, even when your hands are tired and you might want to stop for other reasons.

Then I came to a part of the ritual that I had not thought

about very much. I had to get to the skeleton of the duck to find the right bone. I thought about using the beak, because that is what ducks use to point, but it is not really a bone so it would not work. The proper bone would be somewhere in the duck, like in its leg. The easiest way of getting it out would be to cook it, but of course this would destroy any magic immediately. So I had to cut into it.

When I started doing this I wished I knew more about how the aborigines did it. They probably had the right knives and knew how to hold them properly. I had a knife but it was only a kitchen knife that I use for chopping vegetables. It made a lot of mess and it was a pity because the duck was worth respect and making such a mess was not very respectful. But there was no other way to do it except by cutting.

This took a long time and I am going to skip it because if ever I need another pointing bone this part would put me off. Maybe next time I can think of something better, like leaving the body to be stripped clean by foxes and collecting the bone in the morning. If we lived in the country it would be much easier, because I knew the keepers would find out what I had done if I didn't clear everything up. The feathers were the worst; they went everywhere.

I got the bone. It was from the right leg, the top part. I washed it in the pond in the darkness. All the rest of the duck I put into an old plastic bag I found in the rushes and I tied it really tight. On my way home, when I was safely out of the park, I put the bag into a skip and covered it up with other rubbish.

All the power of that duck was concentrated now into the one bone. I slept with it under my pillow and it gave me dreams like I have never had before. I won't write them down yet, because dreams are not scientific. But they are even better than Micka's dreams.

I feel happier than I have for a long time because at last I am taking control of my life and because I now have a secret source of power. And the bone could be very useful when we kidnap the stray girl. I will tell Micka soon that I have the bone. There is one really good thing about him; I know he will never tell anyone else what we are planning, because he never gives me away at school. And he is the right partner for the kidnap. That day in the park when he said he was sick of it all, that was what gave me the idea of capturing someone and having power over them. And he was excited by it, just the same as I was.

Laurie has been talking about doing some kind of spell from his books, using the magic bone he has got, and I am going to help him. In return he will kill Lee. He says he can do it easy with the bone that will do long-distance magic. He told me I have to get something of Lee's that smells of him.

It is quiet when Lee is away. I heard Mam say he was in London. She is scared he is in trouble because she has no address for him. She thinks he might get done over in London by gangs. No such luck as that. He is too bad to be smashed up like Kevo.

I don't go in Lee's room, but I have to find a thing of his, so I do it quick to get it over. It is still like he has left his eyes to watch you and remember what you do in there. Lee collects things. He has photos of women in a book under his mattress and the pages are stuck together. I tore out one page. It smelt of Lee all right. Laurie said it would be enough; it would make the magic work okay and he said to wait a bit and he would do the magic.

If it is magic, I can't be blamed for it. No one can. Laurie says he will give Lee a quick death. He could do it slow if I wanted, with torture. I said no. Just dead is what he needs. And while he is away in London. Then Mam and Kevo would not know about anything.

My Gran says you should pray. So I pray as well, but I think Laurie has the edge.

We have reached Phase Two. I need to record things more like a scientist. They have phase one, phase two, and so on, and they can compare when each phase is over if they have had any success. I have complete success so far. I know this, because nobody has stopped me. And my plans have definitely not been found out by my parents. Even Micka is only in the part of it that is PHASE FOUR. Sometimes I wonder about my mother, is she outside or not? Sometimes she seems to know more than she lets on. But I think that is because she is doing another experiment of her own that I am outside of.

So I am going to start Phase Three by killing Micka's bad brother Lee. I know that he is scared to death of Lee. And he hates him too. I think I will have to meet Lee face to face soon, so I can test myself and see if he scares me at all.

I am not sure if Micka is a hard man or not. I hope he is.

The day of the bone magic I woke up sick. The fridge is broke and the stew was left over three days. Mam said I could stay off school, but I had to go. Laurie was going to do the stuff with the bone at midnight and I had to know did it work.

He was at school. The bone was in his pocket; he showed it me when we were in the hall singing hymns. When we did the prayer for the day he stroked the bone and he did not do the amen.

~ Did you do the magic yet on Lee?

We were in the line to show Miss Glennie our work books.

~ What do you think?

~ When will - you know - when?

Laurie said real loud, When will he die, you mean?

Miss Glennie looked up from a book.

~ Are you reading Michael your story, Laurie?

~ No, Miss. My pet rabbit is sick.

~ I'm sorry to hear that, but please don't talk while you are waiting.

Laurie is so quick with his talk. How does he think of things that aren't real before a grownup can blink, even. He shoved the bone into my back and it was like the beak of a black crow stabbing in there.

~ Tell you later.

Then he told me in the playground he held the bone over Lee's pictures from the magazine and asked the bone to do its work. But there was something not right that time. The bone should get warm when it is working, and it would not. So Laurie thinks maybe he must kill something else first to give it more strength.

I don't know any more about the bone, if it is bullshit or not. Why do I listen to Laurie? He is only like me; he can't kill Lee any better than me. And he does not know Lee, so it is only a game to him. He has no brothers; he does not know what brothers is like.

But one good thing happened that day. A parcel came for me. It was from Uncle Mikey. To say thanks for the picture I did him. It was a knife. A cool knife, razor sharp. It was Mikey's before he was in prison. He gave it me. I will keep it for ever. It was good he sent it on a day when Lee and Kevo were out. Even Mam does not know where I have hid it.

CHAPTER 7

June

It was time to try it out properly.

I kept it for a whole month and every day I talked to it. I know it is stronger now. It feels good in my hand. I am sure it is heavier than it was and it gets warm very quickly when I hold it.

Micka knows I have done the bone for his brother. He believes in its power. But I don't think its magic is strong enough yet. Maybe I will truly use the bone on Lee after I see it work on something a bit smaller. Lee might get killed in a fight in London first, and then I will tell Micka it was the bone. If I ever said to Micka I had pointed the bone at him, I am pretty sure he would lie down and die like the aborigines. The power of the bone is the power of the mind.

So on this day I was at home and my mother was at the hairdresser's. She knew I should have been at school but she was in one of her moods where she said fuck the system a lot, so I knew she would not care if I did not go. She gave me a cake and a video and said to stay indoors until she got back. The cake was brilliant. It had kirsch in it, which is a kind of alcoholic drink made from cherries. I was not drunk, though, which is a good thing because you cannot work magic if you are drunk.

I got the bone from under my pillow and held it and stroked it until it was warm. The next bit was a sort of accident, but also a kind of brilliant thought that just popped into my head. In my father's bookcase there is a Bible with a green leather cover. It suddenly seemed to jump out at me. I took the Bible out of the bookcase and put it on the carpet. I opened it so the words were all upside down and I stood over it and dropped the bone dead onto the page and it fell exactly on some words. I learned all the words the bone was touching. This will always be part of the bone magic. It has to be upside down because it is not me that chooses the words, it is the bone.

Then I went into the sitting room where the snake was asleep in its cage. I turned on the lamp and pushed it over the cage and held it as close as I could to the coils of the sleeping snake so the warmth would wake it up.

I don't really know why I chose the snake as my first experiment. It was supposed to be my present. It was the first thing my mother gave me after she split up with my father. But I never had any choice about it. It just arrived and I wasn't even here. I think a surprise present like that takes all your power of choosing away and then it is better not to have anything. My mother likes stroking the snake and hissing to it in its language (she says). What she likes best is feeding it with mice and rat pups. It is not true that they have to be alive. You can get them freshly dead from the pet shop. When I feed the snake I hate her watching me. And even though the feel of a snake in your hands is interesting and watching it move around is good fun sometimes, the snake is a cold-hearted creature that does not care about anything, not even about its owner. Snakes are not like dogs, who really show you their feelings. Maybe that is why my mother likes the snake so much, and hates dogs. She is always saying that if she was Prime Minister she would bring in a law that all stray dogs should be rounded up and shot immediately.

As the warm light of the lamp touched the skin of the snake, it slowly uncurled and opened its eyes and for the first time it really looked at me, and its snake brain understood that something special was going to happen to it, and for the first time it saw that I was its true owner and could do what I liked with it. At that exact moment I wished I was not going to use the bone on it, but it was decided already. I could not be sure that tomorrow the snake would look at me again like that. That feeling was just a passing weakness, because when I held the bone over the snake's head as close as I could and said the Bible words, which I will never write down because they are secret and known only to the bone and me, and I shut my eyes and thought as hard as I could about the snake lying dead and stiff in the cage and I felt the bone getting warmer and heavier in my hand and I was squeezing it so hard it felt as if the bone was quivering with its own power. Then I knew what I was doing was strong and right magic.

Afterwards I turned the lamp off and sat by the cage and watched the snake. When the light was off it settled back to sleep. Soon it was very still and I knew that by tomorrow morning it would be dead. The bone had done its work.

I was making a sandwich of all the things in the fridge stacked up on top of each other when my mother came in later with a terrible new hairstyle. Someone at the hairdresser's had told her that she had a few grey hairs and I expect she freaked out completely. She got them to dye her hair. The colour was horrible, sort of a sickly orange. Then they must have put loads of hair gel on and puffed it all out around her head and when she walked in, waggling her head around in a show-off kind of way, I nearly laughed.

~ What do you think, darling?

I did not know what to say. I stared at her for a long time without blinking. She looked like a doll or a clown. Her face seemed extra white. She lit a cigarette and sat in the chair opposite me, and she could go on not blinking longer than I could, so in the end I had to blink first.

~ My sternest critic. Come on. Tell me the truth, darling. I can take it.

~ It looks like a film hairstyle.

This was true, except that I meant a horror film. She was pleased because she thought I was saying she looked like a film star.

There were no fresh dead mice left because she had forgotten to buy any from the pet shop, but before I went to bed she wrote a shopping list and put mice and hair gel on it.

She woke me up early. These days she does not seem to need to sleep at all. She was wearing a black nightie, and with her orange hair all sticking out she looked exactly like a vampire. I don't know why she doesn't take off her make-up before she goes to bed because in the morning her eyes look as if they have been punched.

~ Disaster.

She was standing in the doorway of my room, holding on to the door, and in her other hand was a cigarette.

~ What disaster?

~ Our Beloved Slipperiness has passed away.

~ Are you sure?

~ Don't be upset, darling. He looks very peaceful. I'm sure it was from natural causes.

~ Maybe it was because you forgot to buy the mice.

~ Maybe.

I had to look, to check out if it was true the snake was dead. It was lying just as I had left it yesterday, but when I felt its flesh it was as cold as a dead fish. It was definitely dead. Normally if you try and uncoil it, it tenses its muscles and puts up a fight, but now it let itself be lifted and pulled out straight.

We measured it in centimetres and in feet and inches. It was six feet five inches. Then my mother said, I've been thinking—

~ What about?

~ What you said. Maybe it was my fault. Perhaps it died of hunger because we didn't feed it yesterday.

Grownups will believe anything they want. If she had read about snakes in the encyclopaedia she would know that they do not need to eat every day. Some snakes don't eat for months. But it was good to let her go on thinking that she had killed the snake. It made me feel excited with my power, the same way I did when I bit Polly's fingers at the theatre.

Then my mother asked if I wanted another snake. She said I would have to go to school tomorrow and she could get the snake straight away and it would be waiting for me when I came in. I made her promise she wouldn't get a snake. Or any other pet. The bone would not be pleased to have its work undone in that way.

I went to school. I left the bone under my pillow. Now

I know it works. Quite quickly, too. The bone has made its first kill.

Laurie was off school. Then he came back. He says he is gone from faze2 to faze3. I don't know what faze3 is but I am in faze4.

He said I was to go to his house to see the result of faze2. That is the first time he said I could go to his place.

He opened the front door. There was a lot of colours of glass set in the door. If it was our house they would all be broken with kids chucking stones at the glass. The colours and patterns was like in church. When we went in the hall the light shone through and the carpet was red and blue and green. He pinched my arm to make me stop looking at it and pulled me into a big room. There was a carpet in that room too. It was dark green and soft like a bed of moss.

His mother was not there. Only a smell of her like lipstick in the Galloways shop. We were standing in the room and in the middle there was a glass cage with a dead snake in.

~ Put your hand in. You can touch it.

I touched the skin. It was like Uncle Mikey's face where the scar is. Rough.

~ It's dead. Good and dead.

At school he never told me about killing the snake. I told him things when I had the pup. When it died and all.

~ I killed it. The bone and I. This time yesterday I stood where you are now and held the bone over it like this. I couldn't tell you before because it would weaken the magic.

When Laurie talks like that it sounds like it is real. If other people said it it would sound bullshit but not Laurie.

~ How did you?

~ The bone has come to its full power.

We went in his room. A big room. He has a carpet. The bed is a new kind with cupboards all around. They let him write on his walls; his parents let him write 'fuck school' and stuff. He showed me the place where he keeps the bone under his pillow. But I wasn't to touch, in case I got some of the magic stuff off it.

~ You said you would kill Lee.

~ Maybe I have. Maybe he's dead already.

~ He fucken isn't. And I brought you the fucken pictures and all.

~ That was just a game. Now the bone has killed. Now it has power to kill a human.

~ Can I work it?

~ No. It only does what I tell it.

Laurie is stroking the bone; I get out of his way. He could point at me real easy. He is playing like he is the snake and I the rabbit. I shut my eyes and see Lee again with the yellow worms and he talks but I don't hear the words. Only Lee's mouth says, *You are dead my son.*

149

~ Can you make him go away, like for always?

~ No. Only kill.

~ What about hurt bad?

~ No. Kill or nothing. Fast or slow.

He says it like it is a small little thing to do. I want Lee killed. But I can't say it or the Devil will come after me. And Lee will come after me when he is dead. I want it so bad but I can't ask.

~ If you don't say what you want, I can't help you. You're shit scared. Coward. Wanker. Poof. Sissy.

~ All right. Do it.

~ You have to say it.

~ Do it. Do the killing.

~ I can't hear you. Say it louder. Say, I want Lee killed.

~ I want . . .

The diamond in my belly melting to a red jelly. In my throat the worms swimming, yellow worms.

~ Say it!

~ I fucken am saying! Give me a fucken chance!

~ I'll count to ten.

Laurie is real calm and quiet. He is looking at me same as old Babs looks.

~ If you don't ask me by then, you've lost your chance.

~ Okay. Do it! Use the bone. Kill Lee.

~ Too late. I counted.

~ You never.

150

~ I did, in my head.

Laurie puts the bone back in his pocket. He made me say it so the Devil heard, but now he won't do it. I try and take the bone off him but he starts kicking me good and we fight and I lose. He points his finger at my heart and he says,

~ So now you'll take me to Royts Lane and then I'll kill Lee with the bone. Otherwise – you lose.

I always lose with Laurie.

It seems like I am in control. Micka thinks so. Just after he came round to my house and saw the bone, his brother Lee came back. This time he did not send any postcard before like he does usually. He arrived one morning and Micka said he smelled of drink but he was no bother. He went straight to bed and slept for two days and they all had to be very quiet.

When he woke up he was in a good mood, Micka says. He gave their mother fifty pounds to buy a buggy for the baby, which he had never done before. It seems he quite likes the baby so he is being nicer to their mother. But he is still the same to Micka. So Lee is next for the bone.

We made a plan that I would see Lee. It is the only way. The bone cannot kill someone as strong as Lee by remote control. I asked Micka where could we go so I could see Lee without him seeing me. Micka said he is down the

Black Badger pub a lot, so we said we would meet there at half-past ten tonight. There is a good window we could look in at which is quite low down.

This pub is in a very bad part of town, the kind of pub my father would pull me past very quickly in case I saw anyone drunk coming out. Although he likes vodka, he only drinks at home which is, he says, the civilised way to drink.

Micka looked cool leaning up against the wall of the pub and I went and leant next to him.

~ He's inside.

I tried to look in but someone was standing up inside with their back pressed against the window.

~ It's darts night. Full house.

~ We'll have to go in then.

~ Na, he'll see us. I'm not.

~ You have to; I don't know which one he is.

~ He looks like a con and he has a belt with a wolf head on it.

~ Okay, if you're chicken.

I went in the small door of the bar. It was really hard to see anything with the smoke and all the men standing in front of me. I tapped one and asked if I could use the toilet. He pointed down the other end of the bar and I wriggled and squeezed my way through and I smiled a sickly smile when some of them made jokes about my bladder must be bursting and how many pints had I had.

I looked as hard as I could and all I could see were loads of men who could be Lee. When men are sitting down, you can't really see their belts at all. I was holding the bone in my pocket so hard it felt red hot, but there was no point in using it here.

After I had gone to the toilet I came back. Micka was still there, leaning up against the wall and biting his nails. When he saw me his skinny face lit up like a kid waiting for Christmas.

~ Did you see him, did you?

~ How could I? Millions of bloody Lees in there. At least I went in.

~ Don't go. He'll come out in a minute.

~ Why should he come out? There's ages to go before closing time, wanker.

~ He does it all the time. Comes out with someone, they talk and then he goes back in.

~ Well, if he comes out, he'll see you. Won't he belt you or something?

~ He won't do nothing out here.

I said I would wait twenty minutes.

For once Micka was right. The door opened and three men came out and they were shouting. At first I thought it was a row, then I saw they were laughing. One of them had a paper and he was showing the other two a picture but when they tried to look he took it away.

~ That's him. Micka's lips didn't even move; he nodded at the one who was doing the teasing and laughing the loudest and I knew it was Lee. He was taller than I thought and his hair was black and quite long.

Then he saw us and he stopped laughing in the very next second and he came up to Micka and pushed him hard against the wall.

~ So what you doing here, ye little cunt ye? Get home.

~ I'm going.

Lee did not let go of Micka; his hand was so big he could hold him up against the wall of the pub by the throat. His thumb was touching the wall on one side and all his fingers on the other side. Micka has got a neck as thin as a turkey and he swallowed and Lee's hand didn't shift a fraction of a bit.

~ You spying on us?

~ No I swear to God we—

~ We?

Lee spun round and took in that I was standing there and in the dark his face seemed to get actually darker red in colour and his friends started pulling him back but he shook them off and reached with his long arm towards me, only I jumped out of the way.

~ And who are you?

~ Didn't Micka tell you, Lee? I'm the Devil.

I thought it sounded good calling him by his name, but Micka's eyes went round and huge and he tried to shake his head and the next minute Lee had sprung back from the wall and belted me as hard as he could on the side of my face and while I stopped dead still, he followed up with a punch to my guts and while I was staring at the pavement as it spun round and round under my eyes he spoke softly into my ear.

~ Take the piss out of me my son and you are fucking dead.

Then a woman came out of the bar. She was wearing tight black trousers and as I put my head up all I could see was a massive tight belt made of some shiny silver material. Not metal, like Lee's belt. She had on a pink blouse and the front was open right down to her tits.

~ Are you playing darts or what? she said. She was smiling at Lee like she liked him. He grabbed hold of her by her front and kissed her and she closed her eyes and Lee's two friends stood laughing and saying rude things and they had forgotten all about us. Then Lee stopped kissing her and she pulled him back in the pub by his belt and the others went in after him.

After they had gone, I felt it hurt more. But it was strange how it almost didn't hurt enough. The punch could have been harder. I could have taken it. That is my power. I stood up straight and Micka was waiting like the donkey and the ox in the stable and his rabbit eyes were staring at me till I moved.

~ Now you know how he is. No one can stand up to him, no one.

~ I bloody can, I bloody well can. Who was that woman?

~ Lee's new slag. She won't last, he'll hit her too. He's too strong. Nobody can beat Lee.

~ Oh, *shut up*.

I started walking home and he followed just behind. All I wanted was to get home and think hard and do the magic while I still had the power of Lee and his badness on me, but Micka's voice was taking it all away. Micka's feet paddling along behind me stopped the power of the magic and made me feel like a baby, wanting to cry. I turned around suddenly and pushed him away.

~ Go home.

~ But the bone stuff?

~ Go home.

~ But will you do it?

~ I don't know. I don't know anything if you keep on and on at me. Go fucking home.

~ He'll kill me when he gets in.

~ That's your lookout.

~ Kill him tonight; will you kill him before he leaves the pub?

~ It doesn't work like that, I told you.

~ If I take you to Royts Lane will you?

At last he began to back off and I stopped and waited till he had gone and then I went home.

When I got home I looked in the mirror and for all the beating there wasn't a mark on me. Lee is an expert, and for that I admire him. But he is also a bully and for that I will point the bone. But Lee has some other force, so it probably won't work like it did with the snake. Lee has seen lots of people look him in the eye who would like him to be dead and it rolls off him like the water off a duck's back. I think that is what is called a proverb. I think I showed no fear to him. Although it is good that I don't ever have to meet him again.

Just before I fell asleep I had a brilliant thought. The bone would work better on Lee if it could kill someone else first. A human being, someone small and weak. Any human being. Then I can do it properly on Lee.

Lee did not come home that night. He went with his new slag. Mam says she will get Lee into bad trouble.

Paula has a real good smile now. She smiles at me. She does not cry much. Lee says she is a great little tart. Lee likes her. Does he know about Donna, I wonder?

Kevo has a job cleaning windscreens. He has to get up early to get to the best pitch by the traffic lights before the homeless man comes. One time he was too late and he nearly got into a fight with the homeless man and his mates. But he is still not looking for trouble, so he came home.

CHAPTER 8

July

~ Look.

Blue was pointing. We looked.

It was the field. The grass short and green like a pool table, smooth as far as you could go with your eyes. Where Babs had done her shits was clean, no papers or rubbish there. All over the field was little white and green dots.

~ What are those?

~ Tents.

Blue got over the fence.

~ They came this morning. Must be a hundred or more. Crazy people, they are. Two big coaches and cars, and they've lit a big fire and they're digging like moles, all over the field. It's mad.

~ Are they soldiers? Laurie was over the fence so quick he ripped his jeans.

~ Na. Kids.

~ Are they travellers, then? I said. I saw them far off, little moving black dots. Laurie spat on the grass.

~ Just a bunch of boy scouts. Wankers.

Blue ran ahead so fast I couldn't keep up with him. Laurie stayed back. His mouth was in a twist. He didn't want to go with us.

~ You don't have to come.

He fetched me a punch in the back that made my eyes water.

~ Fuck off.

We walked on. Came to a boy. He was digging with a pick. He was all covered in dirt and his hair was long and conker colour and falling all the time in his eyes. There was two other boys lying in the grass slagging him, the way he held the pick. Then they saw us.

~ Are you Kestrels? one said. He was a black kid, spoke posh.

~ No, are you wankers? Laurie bust his gut laughing.

~ Then bugger off, said the digging boy. It sounded wrong with his voice so posh.

~ This is the Kestrels' lat.

~ The what? said Laurie.

One of the boys lying on the grass said, Don't you know what a lat is? It's where we shit.

The long hair boy dropped the pick.

~ It's your go, Sam.

Laurie was licking his lips and smiling his bad smile. I knew what he was waiting for, for the kids to dig so he could laugh at them and they would give up.

~ Give it here.

Blue took the pick and started to dig. He never gave a toss about Laurie. Laurie sat on the grass on the other side of the pit. The digging boy sat down.

~ So, who are you? If you're not Kestrels, who are you?

~ Are you from London?

These kids all talked the same, it was rough the way they talked but the sound was posh. Not like we talk.

~ Did you come on the coach, because I didn't notice you? said the last one. His head was shaved all right but he had a softy voice and his jeans were new.

Laurie said, Do you smoke?

Long hair boy nodded.

~ Give us one, then. Be a good boy scout and do your good turn.

~ Fuck you, we're not scouts, said the black one. He was the poshest one. We are Earth Tribe People. We don't have fucking stupid rules like scouts do. And if you're not with us, you shouldn't be here.

~ Thought you didn't have rules, poof, said Laurie. The black one stood up.

~ You've got a big mouth, smartarse. Why don't you let your dumb friends talk for a change?

Laurie grabbed some soil and threw it in his eyes. He roared and kicked back a load of soil over Laurie's face and in his hair and I laughed but not with any sound. Laurie was pushing the boy down in the trench, then he got the shovel and started covering him up with loads of soil.

~ Fucking bury you ... Laurie was in a rage like I have never seen him but his voice went dead quiet, like Mikey. The boy rose up out the trench, with the black earth scattering all over us like a dog fresh out of the water scatters the drops, then he grabbed Laurie by the throat and then we were all fighting, me and Laurie against the other three, kicking mostly. Blue backed off. He was still holding the pick. Laurie yelled at him to use the pick but he still backed off. I got cut over my eye and the blood was everywhere. The fight stopped. Softy one said, I'm not getting your fucking blood on my new 501s.

~ Anyway here comes the staff, said the big one and they all started digging double fast like they were slaves on a chain gang.

~ No rules, huh? Laurie was breathing heavy from the fight but he folded his arms real cool and smiled his red fox smile. Here comes your babysitter ...

~ Get lost, pervert, said the long hair one. Laurie was laughing. A man and a woman came. They looked at me and Laurie real hard. The woman said, That's a nasty cut, how did you get that? Before I could run she got to me and held my face in her hands and looked hard into my face. Her hands smelled of soap.

She loosed her hands a minute and I pulled away. She looked at the man with her. He said, Come on, what happened? He was not roaring and he had no belt in his jeans. The black boy said, Nothing, only the spade slipped.

Blue was nowhere. He knows to keep away from bother. Then they started at me again.

~ You're too small to be a Kestrel, what group are you in?

~ What's your name, you may be on a list—

~ Go to the first-aid tent and get that eye seen to, it's the big green tent over there—

~ Have you put your tents up yet? You have to do that before dinner—

Laurie pulled on my arm and whispered without his lips moving, let's fuck off. We walked towards the big tent until the woman and man weren't looking after us, then we switched around on our track and ran back to the traveller site.

Blue was waiting by the trailer. Laurie pointed at my face, the blood.

~ Micka's not a fucking chicken. He didn't run off.

Blue stared at Laurie with no blinking.

~ Why did you run off like a girl? Why didn't you use the pick, you fucking gyppo?

Blue kept staring and he never blinked once.

~ Say something, Laurie said. He took a step toward Blue. Blue did not move.

~ I don't fight other men's battles.

Blue turned and walked into the trailer. We was left standing. My eye cut hurt bad. Laurie gave me a push.

~ Slippery. That's what gypsies are. He's supposed to be your friend? Waste of space.

~ I never wanted you to come.

~ Wanker.

I sat on a box and Laurie started to light the fire. Blue came out the trailer with bread and jam for us. He gave some to Laurie even. I was going to chuck it on the fire but Blue ate it and smiled at me and he was okay and never got sick and I was hungry so I ate it anyway. Then we sat around the fire till it was dark. Blue had a blanket wrapped around him like an old Indian.

Then Babs came back from town and she got some water and she washed the cut and the blood off my face. Blue was still. I wondered where was his mother and father. Laurie kept kicking the fire.

In the dark of the night there was a red glow in the sky over the field. We all saw it. And heard the noise like rushing of waves on a stony beach. Blue stood up and threw off the blanket.

~ I'm going back.

Babs fussed and told him no, but he never minded her.

We went back to the fence and got over and walked dead quiet into the field. In the dark it smelled ripe and rich of grass just cut.

The glow in the sky was from a big fire. The rushing noise got louder and it was the sound of all of them singing. They did not see us come up. Laurie whispered to me, If there were more of us we could attack them now. They wouldn't stand a chance.

They were sitting in a big circle around the fire, maybe a hundred or more of kids and grownups, and their faces were all looking into the flames and they were as smooth and pink as little babbies.

There was a space on a big log and we sat in. No one told us to go. The small kids were sitting around flashing their pissy little torches. There were even some girls in it. And the men with beards and dressed with big green jackets like it was winter and raining and all but it was summer. Some women were there with long hair, loose and blowing in the smoke of the fire. And babies, walking around on their own, falling over sometimes. When they cried, someone took them up.

Laurie got a long branch and stuck it in the fire till it was red. He pulled it out and a beardy man said, Hey, pal, what's your name?

Laurie said, Bobby. Then he cracked up laughing.

~ Okay, Bobby, we don't play around with fire in the Earth Tribe People because someone could get hurt, okay?

Blue looked like he wasn't going to move. Laurie was looking for trouble. I was stuck in the middle.

That's how it was with us three together.

That boy, Blue, is asking for a hiding. He is asking to have the bone tried out on him. Micka makes out he is so nice and his life is so great going out with the pickup and begging for stuff with the men, but he seems dopey and a bit slow in the head to me. You can't trust him – he is slippery like everyone says gypsies are, and he never lifted a finger to help me in the fight with the Earth Tribe kids. Micka must be partly a tinker himself, I think. Otherwise why would he love squatting down by Babs' filthy old fire watching her spit in the flames?

I think people who live like that are no better than animals. I think they deserve what they get. And it is time the bone was used on a person. There really is not anyone else who will do as my next victim.

I decided to go to the gypsy site at night and point the bone at Blue when he was asleep. If the bone is truly effective, it will do its work whether he knows about it or not. It may not work, but even if it does, he is only one stupid gypsy and I am sure there are others there who could be just as good friends with Micka. Even so, it is a good idea not to tell Micka any of this. I think he might give me a hard time if he knew what I was going to do to his friend.

I need to write this down for the next time I use the bone. This is what I did. I went to the gypsy site alone. It was the night after we had the fight with the camping kids.

I made the bone warm with my spit while I was standing outside the trailer where Blue sleeps. I looked in and there was no one else there but Blue and he was asleep with the light on.

I pointed the bone at him through the window and I shut one eye and moved the point of the bone until it was lined up with his heart and I whispered, There. Then I moved the bone until it was lined up with his brain and I said, There. Then I moved the bone to his belly but his hand was resting there, so maybe the bone was pointing at his hand and I said, There.

Three places are enough. I went home and no one saw me.

Laurie will not come to Royts Lane with me now. He hates the place. But that is okay because it was never his place. Anyway he says he is busy with ideas, he has plenty. He is like a pirate chief. In the park he said we had to be blood brothers and he cut our fingers and we put the blood together and said brothers till death parts us, and after that he gave me a letter done up with string and red stuff you

167

cannot break. I was not to open it ever, except in case of death. If I opened it he said the magic with Lee would not work, but if I left it, Lee would for sure be no more trouble to me by the end of school holidays. He says he would never lie to me now we have done the blood brother thing. Maybe – but what is so good about brothers? Blood or any kind, all are shite.

It is good Laurie doesn't come to Royts Lane any more. Blue is too much the quiet man when Laurie is around.

I went back the day the camping people were packing up to go home. All running about the field like ants and still digging like moles. And so much shouting from the men and women that we knew to keep clear from it.

Blue was going fishing in the canal. He had fixed a line and a hook and he made one just as good for me. We had a big old bucket and a net. We went to the canal where the broken wall is and climbed over and there was a good place to sit on an old log above the water. Babs had done us a picnic tied in a blue cloth with bread and cheese and some biscuits and a big bottle of fizzy lemon. And I didn't care about her shitting or the dirt because this is the way life comes with Blue and it is okay.

The day was a hot day and the way it went on was slow and like in a dream, only not a bad dream. There was sun and later the sun went below the shade of a big tree of small leaves, Blue says an ash tree, and the soft lights of the sun on the canal water through the small leaves was here and there darting like fishes and the water drinking in the sun like it was the fizzy stuff and no one came to bother us. There was not much words spoken. Blue shares without pushing it in my face all the time; he is not like Laurie.

In my pocket was the silver thing the police gave me on Christmas. I never used it. I got it out and showed it to Blue.

~ My Uncle Joey plays one like this. Mouth organ, he calls it.

Blue gave it a blast and it made the sound of a chicken squawk and we bust our shite laughing. I said he could keep it. He said he would get his Uncle to teach him how to play.

When the sun was low my line tangled. I pulled and pulled and a big metal spring came up on the end of the line and it had mud all over from the canal bottom. I was cursing and I pulled it a good one and it came free and the spring fell on Blue but I did not mean to do it. He does not get in a rage when things go like that. He started to get the hook free of the spring but it cut his hand. There was mud and blood mixed on his hand and he was wiping it on his shirt and that was when I thought of my bad dream again. I went away along the path and kept my eyes open but all I could see was the fish that talked lying in the bucket with the baby eyes all red. I ran back and he was sitting just like before with his rod and line and his hand still red.

~ Don't fish any more, Blue. Let's do something else.

~ I can't go yet. I haven't caught even one. I can't go home with nothing.

~ Blue, man, the dream. Remember the dream? I told Babs. She said it was bad luck. About the fish. Maybe this was it.

But he had forgot the dream.

I did not want to stay so I left the line and hook and all and went home. Blue stayed there in the evening sun, still fishing. He is like a man, how he sits and waits and thinks by himself. I wonder where is his Mam and Dad. Is Babs all his family? He never asks me who is my family. This is the way gypsies go on. I like the way they go on.

The next time I went back to Babs's trailer, Blue was not there. I asked her what about him and she said he was moved to Joey Connors' trailer, it is bigger, because Blue is sick and he is in bed. And there is a stove in Joey's trailer and it is not broke like Babs' stove.

~ Can I go see him?

~ No. He's too sick for visitors. If he gets any worse now we'll be fetching the doctor to him.

~ What's wrong with him?

~ He got a deep cut on his hand.

~ How did he get sick from a cut?

Babs fixes me with her eye.

~ The cut went bad. The bad went into his blood. It's all through his poor body now, so it is. Pray for him.

She had a tear ready to fall along her cheek. She did not

want me there. So I went to Joey Connors' big flash trailer and there was a crowd of them sitting around outside by a fire that was of small coals. I stood at the back of them. They passed a bottle around them. I wondered was any of them Blue's Mam or Dad. One saw me and said, Go home, gorgio boy.

~ I want to see Blue. I got something for him.

The man stuck out his hand for the thing. It was the Romany man with the black tongue gave me the bad pup. I had nothing. I put my hands behind my back.

~ No. I want to give it to Blue.

~ He's too sick. He won't know you. That was a woman spoke, with long red hair and a red coat. She was young. Could his Mam be that young one? He is only the same age as me. I tapped her on the shoulder.

~ Will he go to the hospital?

They don't talk to me. They start arguing with themselves about the hospital and call a doctor and I can't get near the trailer and the noise of them shouting is like a fight and so I go.

Next day I go back and no one is there. I try the door of Babs' trailer and it is shut and she has fixed the lock some way that I can't open it. I get a box and stand on the box and look in. No one. The bed is empty Blue used to sleep in. On the table is dirty plates and cups and butts like they left in a hurry. I walk around the site. Only four trailers left.

Some have gone since yesterday. Joey Connors' trailer is still there but locked.

I wait a while but no one comes. I walk along home by the canal. The hook cut his hand. Mud and blood mixed. Blue sitting, fishing, thinking. Like a man.

Next day I didn't go. But that night I dreamed the fish dream and Blue was there. He was standing by the bucket with his hand in where the fish lay. His head was half eaten with maggots, his half of a mouth was smiling at me. He took the fish and put it in his mouth and bit and then I woke up. I had to make myself awake. The dream is the worst thing in my life. I have to wake up every time before it ends.

So I went back. I did not want to go but I had to know was Blue going on okay.

Everything was different again. There was more trailers there. Old Babs was sitting outside her trailer and the fire was going. I waited for her to see me. She was whispering to herself and her hands was ashy.

~ Where's Blue? Is he better?

~ He passed away. In the hospital. Blue passed away.

It was like in my gut I knew it anyway. But for my mind to know it needed more words. When she said the words there was like a flash of grey over the day and the site and then it was gone and the site came back and the fire and Babs and the ashy light was all around us.

~ Can I stay?

She lifted her shoulders and shrugged her head on one side like Mam does when life is too hard. I stayed. We sat for a long time with no words spoke. Babs was his Nan. I sat on a box next her, where Blue used to sit sometimes. The fire did not warm us hardly at all. I put more wood on. The day was cold. Babs came awake a bit when the flames were red. She was talking in a sort of a dream with herself only, even her eyes when they looked toward me did not see me.

~ I was sitting with him when they took him. We got in the ambulance and he was very bad. His heart stopped beating. The ambulance men put the wires on his chest and he bumped up once and fell back down. They told me to keep away from him. They did it again, then I held his hand and felt for his pulse and his heart was beating for a moment like a sparrow chick under the claw of a cat. I knew then it was over, and only myself there that knew the boy. When we got to the hospital his mother was there, they brought her from town, Joey Connors' lads in the van. He never knew us again after, though we sat by his bed all that day and the night. He was in a coma. They say he was not in pain, thank God. We stayed and at five o'clock in the morning he passed on.

I said in my head, *Blue was a good man. The good men die.*

~ And now they're coming, from all over. Look at the wagons, the trailers. The O'Briens from Ireland and the Townsleys from Perth. All her family. There'll be more here

173

by tonight. Hundreds maybe. Like in the old days. Maybe even his Daddy will show his face, the skiting weasel.

We stayed sitting and the fire stopped leaping with flames and died to red ashes, and we had no heart to put on more wood.

Then a man came from Joey Connors' trailer with a cardboard box.

~ This is his stuff.

He put the box down. I saw Blue's clothes in there. Babs gave a nod to the man.

~ Throw them on the fire.

The man did not.

~ Will we not wait on Bridie herself?

Babs shook her head.

~ Everything to be burnt. Or his spirit cannot go free. Would you bind him forever to this place?

The man backed off. Then people came running and I saw the woman with the red hair and the red coat drive up in a truck with two men and the man ran shouting to her and they came to Babs' fire, shouting and roaring and I got inside Babs' trailer and watched through the window.

~ Is this true what he says? The woman was screaming and I saw by the set of her mouth and the shape of her eyes she was Blue's mother.

~ You've burnt everything of my boy's? Before I had even a chance—

She took Babs by the collar of her coat and shook her and there was fighting all around and women screaming and crying and in the fight the box of clothes was kicked over and I saw the clothes Blue was wearing the day he got the cut.

Some of them was pulling at the clothes, some was trying to throw them on the fire. His jeans caught light. Then all the clothes went alight. His check shirt, his socks, his trainers, his small leather belt and all. Last of all they threw out of the box the little silver thing I gave him. The mouth organ. It was in the fire, gone.

Babs and the woman in the red coat was hugging and crying and all the others stood around watching the clothes burning and there was no place for me. I went from the trailer and no one saw me go.

Blue was gone. They had to burn all his things so he could go wherever it is dead gypsies go.

The next day when I went back, all the trailers were gone.

CHAPTER 9

August

The council took back Royts Lane gypsy site and put up a fence with a big gate and a padlock so no travellers could come on the place any more. After the campers were gone there was a fair that came in the field and Royts Lane was opened up again for the fair. It was the second time we had a fair, but last year it was on Spital Moor.

Laurie said it would be there for two weeks and his Dad would give him twenty pounds and if he felt like it he would give me five.

The fair was all over where Blue's trailer used to be. I saw them putting up the penny roller stall and at the side was the bit of grass where Babs' trailer was, all around it the grass was gone but underneath it always went on growing while Blue and his Nan were in the trailer. Where Babs' fire was, a candy floss stall was put up. I knew where to look for the black earth and the ash stamped into the ground by all the feet of the fair people and I wondered where did his Nan and his Mam and Joey Connors and all go.

Last year Gran took me. Mam would not go, she hates the fair. Gran is too old for the rides but she watched me on the spinning thing. I went twice and I got sick. Gran put my head in the water trough where the ponies are, round the back of the wagons and a woman there with two Alsatians gave me a drink of Coke. Maybe she knew Gran. Gran would not stay then, she dragged me home and said I wasn't to tell what happened. I asked:

~ About the woman, you mean? Or getting sick.

~ About anything. You mind yourself.

This year Gran is not here. And now Mam has the baby she has no time for me. I asked Laurie was he going with the money from his Dad. He said he had twenty pounds but I wasn't getting any, no use begging. I said, I never beg.

~ You do, you beg all the time.

~ I never.

~ Anyway, I'm going with someone else.

I know he is lying, he has no one else. But the money is real enough, he showed me.

Anyway I went to Royts Lane; there was nowhere else to go. And no one can stop you getting in to the fair and hanging around and I watched them all. There was the same kind of kids with their Dads and Mams that I saw at Christmas in the line to see Santy. Eating big candy floss, getting pennies for the penny arcade. One girl dropped her candy floss and it stuck on her coat and her Mam hit her, not much of a hit, and she bawled and roared till her Mam gave her another 50p. Some life for some. I watched there until the candy floss man told me to push off and I watched until it got dark and all the little kids went home. Then the boyfriends and girlfriends came along and they were in a real good mood and sometimes they gave me money if I asked. No one called it begging. One was like Kevo with the same hair and he gave me some chips. And I waited until it was real dark but no Laurie.

I went home and no one was there. Mam goes out a lot with the baby, it drives her mad at nights with the crying so she goes down the Windmill Pub and leaves it in the corridor if I am not home to mind it. I will get a belt for not coming home so she could go out, but so fucken what.

Kevo is sleeping in Lee's bed so I had the bed to myself. Lee is never home these days. I think he is screwing his new slag we saw at the Badger pub so he is not home much, which is good. But when he comes back it will be worse because she will have thrown him out and he will take it out on me.

Gran does not write any more. Maybe Uncle Mikey has died of the AIDS.

One time Mikey told me it did not matter the flat was a kip if you keep the sky in your head. Blue was like that. He had the sky in his head. It would be good to live without a house getting in the way of your sky.

After that night at the fair I was lying in bed looking at the room. The ceiling of the room is yellow. I hate that colour the most of all. There is a mark, a brown shape like a tiger with brown stripes jumping across the room towards me, but it has no legs. It has a jaw wide open and I can see the teeth of it, but then it ends. I wish I did not live here. I wish Mam would paint this place.

So the next night I went back to the fair again and watched. This time I was lucky. Laurie came and he was by himself. He did not see me hiding. I stayed behind him and watched what he did. He went on the rifle range and I watched did he win anything, but he was crap. I had to stop myself from laughing. He had three goes on it and he never hit the bullseye once. Kevo and Lee are dead shots on the rifle range. Lee is best.

I saw Laurie looking at the spinner but you need two people in the car. I wondered should I walk along, but then I saw he was not looking at the spinner, but at something else.

There was a little girl and she was standing watching the spinner and her Mam and Dad were getting on and leaving her behind. First she was waving and she was smiling and jumping up and down all the while they were still in the car, not moving. Then it started to move and her Daddy and

Mammy went away high up in the sky and she looked like she would cry, her mouth was all squashed up. The spinner got real fast and I saw Laurie slowly, slowly, walk nearer to her. She was rubbing her face. Her Mam and Dad were waving but it was all too fast and dizzy to see them. Laurie got down low, he bent down and he started talking to her and she stopped rubbing her eyes. He had something in his pocket and he got it out and gave it to her. She opened it up and it was candy or something and she started sucking on it. And I saw Laurie was smiling his real bad smile.

This was the time I came over to him. I said, Who's this?

~ Her name's Shelley, he says with this bad bad smile and a soft voice, not like his voice when he talks to me. And the girl is holding out her hand to him and he takes it and says,

~ Wave to your Mam, there she is.

~ What's going on with you, Laurie?

~ Research.

Then the spinner stops and they get out and come running to Shelley and say thank you what a kind big boy to Laurie for keeping her happy and he stands there smiling and smiling and Shelley goes with her Mam and Dad and keeps turning round to wave at Laurie so I punch him one to take the smile off his face.

~ I watched you. You were shite on the rifle range.

I thought he would thump me but he shook his head only.

Then he put his hand in his pocket and pulled out some money.

~ You thought I was shite, let's see you do better.

I had two goes but I didn't win. It was with Laurie all the time whispering in my ear about his plan.

~ I know how to do it now, Thicko, he says, and I'm not sure you're going to be in on it because you have no ideas and I have it all worked out, and I think it would be better fun if I do it by myself.

~ Do what?

~ Don't you remember anything, Thicko? Don't you remember what we said?

I whacked his shoulder with the rifle and the man took it off me and told me to piss off.

If he calls me Thicko again he will be sorry. We have done the blood brother thing and made the plan for the kidnap and he is wrong. He is not so clever. He needs me in it.

It was good that the letter was already open and in a place where I could find it. It was in the bathroom by my mother's toothbrush and it was quite wet.

~ Dear Mrs. Parkhurst, it said (not even the right name), This is to let you know that there is definitely a place for your son Laurie starting in the autumn term as we agreed on the phone . . .

The address was somewhere in Sussex. I know that is hundreds of miles away. As far away from our house as you can get. The letter had a fancy heading. The Oliver Tressell Boarding School For Boys. For boys. A boarding school without even any girls. How long had she been planning this? And what about him? Saying he believed in being honest with me about everything.

That day he came round when Josie was cutting up the dress, they were not having a discussion, they had already made up their minds, to send me away, but she would not tell me. She didn't care or she didn't have the guts. And he went along with it.

I didn't cry when I read the letter. Someone else might have cried. I put it back carefully in the same wet patch it was in and it looked exactly as if no one had touched it. When I came home that night it was gone.

They are getting rid of me. That is why Brian has been telling me stories recently about how he loved his boarding school. I suppose I am lucky they waited all this time. He was sent away when he was only six. This was her experiment too. I am just a nuisance to her. However much she smiles at me and lets me stay up till one o'clock and says she doesn't care about me not going to school and how I am nearly a man. It is only because soon she will be shutting me up for weeks at a time.

They lied and lied to me for months, and there is no

one I can tell because they are in charge of me. You can't be rescued from your own parents. I should have learned from the tree accident. Everyone lies to you. Everyone lets you fall.

We don't have much time. We have to do the plan before they send me away. It seems like the thing must happen while the fair is on, which is maybe too soon but if we don't do it now we never will and things could not be worse than they are now. Micka's brother Lee has come back, so the bone has not worked yet. I know he has been belting Micka but I guess that is how things are in his family. I don't think Micka is hard at all. It is only that he never smiles that makes him seem tough.

It has to be soon, while the fair is on. Laurie is right. If we are going to do this plan it has to be soon.

When I think about the plan I think about Lee's belt and last Christmas Day and I want to be in it, I have to be in it. Pressing in on my head are the pictures. The gang who mashed up Kevo's face and Kevo's knife and fork going up and down on the plate and Uncle Mikey dying of the AIDS and the baby Paula drinking the beer from her bottle that Kevo gave her and the pup that died in its shite with its paws chewed off and the dream of the fish and Blue with the mud in the cut on his hand.

Then I know Laurie is right and the plan has to happen at the fair. There has to be an end to all this. The plan will change things.

I know we are blood brothers. But part of my power is that I must not tell Micka all the things I have done and things I am planning. The letter with the sealing wax is a way of telling and not telling. It seals him in with me, but he doesn't know exactly how. Which is deceitful, but necessary.

After the kidnap. I have thought about this. I know Micka hasn't. I know how to talk my way out of trouble; but I need someone with me that people are more likely to notice and remember. Micka has red hair, which is very noticeable, and he is always hanging around the fair, so a lot of the fair people know him already. Afterwards I know he won't be able to lie as well as me.

We have never said out loud exactly what we will do. Which is good. So maybe we will get away with it. Maybe just kidnap the stray girl and hurt her a bit and let her go, and no one will know it was us. Maybe Micka will do more things than me. He has had things done to him by his family he won't tell me. I would be interested to hear his ideas, but the trouble is, he doesn't like talking about ideas in the same way that I do. I know there are things going on in his head. I don't think he is stupid. I want to see what he does. And I want him to watch what I do. That's why we must both be in it.

So, Laurie got ten pounds. His Dad would give him another twenty at the weekend; this ten pounds was from his Mam.

We went on Monday around the middle of the day when the sun was too hot and most things was closed. Laurie says to go at night when all the lights are on, and all the rides are open.

The ghost train was the only thing that was open. Laurie paid me in. He wanted to sit in the car on his own. I went in the car behind. When the car started to move I thought of Blue's ghost and I went to get out but Laurie turned himself in his seat and he gave me a look and I knew if I got out he would slag me and not pay me in for anything else, so I stayed sitting.

I hate the dark, specially alive dark like this was, people moving in it and voices whispering. Not just the skeletons which were only painted, but there was dark shapes in the dark shaking things and maybe turning knobs to make the screaming noises and all the while the train was going faster and faster and around corners real fast so if you did not hold on you would get spun out into the dark and all of a sudden this light comes on and a body all in bandages with a screaming mouth sits up in bed with all wires and blood coming out from the bandages and a look in his eye and I knew it was Blue and I started screaming and a slimy thing touched my face and a cobweb came up at me with a big soft thing with legs hanging down and I got down on the floor of the train and I blocked my eyes and my ears and still in my mind I saw the face of the thing in bandages and I only wanted it to be over.

When I came out I got back on the seat so Laurie did not see. He was standing up in the car and he had stripped off his shirt and his chest was bare and he had stood like that with the spider and cobwebs touching his skin and his hair was dusty like he had been sweeping the ceiling.

~ That was crap. Wasn't it?

~ Yeh.

~ Not scary at all. Was it?

~ No.

~ Liar, you were scared shitless.

~ So were you.

~ I stood up all through. Bet you didn't.

~ The paintings was shite. Of the ghosts and that. I could do better.

~ Yeah, with Miss Glennie helping you.

We fought. Laurie was cold, his shirt was tied around his waist. I couldn't grab hold to kick him a good one, his skin was too tough and slippery. You can grab the skin of fat

186

people or babies easy enough. Laurie is not fat, he is big and all muscle.

~ Don't cry, sissy. I won't make you go on the scary ghost train any more.

He did not wait for me, he ran off too fast for me to catch him. I thought it was not worth it, staying with him in that mood.

I walked about a bit but the smell of the hot dogs was driving me crazy. I watched a dad with his son, feeding him hot dogs. The kid was wearing a green jacket and he would run away a little and turn and run back and take a bite of the roll and run away laughing. Sometimes the Dad would catch hold of the hood of his jacket and pull him back. Then the hot dog was finished and the kid ran and ran around the corner and I lost him. His Dad chucked the paper in a bin and ran quick and came back carrying the kid in his arms tight like there might be danger. He did not shout at him or belt him for running off. He bought a Coke for his kid and they shared it and he stayed holding the kid in his arms and I saw the fat man serving the hot dogs smiling like he had wet himself. There was sandwiches and rolls there in a plastic case but the counter was too high to nick any out.

I was tired and I sat down. Laurie came back. He was in a better mood. He won a blue teddy on the rifles, only a small one.

~ You can have this for your sister.

I wished I had stayed with Laurie and maybe he would have paid me in for a go on the rifles. When Kevo had his airgun he would let me use it sometimes. I liked the aiming part. I did not like it so much when you hit a bird and it dragged its wing and you had to stamp on it. Kevo was dead good at that.

Laurie bought two hot dogs and gave one to me. We sat on an old oil drum. He had a bit of a broken bottle and we scratched our names on the drum and it made like a screeching noise with the glass on the metal.

~ This fair is giving me an idea, Laurie said. You know what I am talking about?

I felt a squeezing in my belly like something heavy was trying to pull it down through my gut. After the hot dog the squeezing made me feel sick. But he was right. The fair was the best place to do the plan.

Laurie was licking his lips like a fox.

~ This fair is the ideal place for a kidnap. When it's this busy it would be really easy to get a child to come away with us. Then we could pretend it was our little sister or brother. We could do it easier here than in the park.

That was the plan before. To steal a kid in the park. Take it away to a secret place. Just to have taken a kid that was small and didn't know anything and could not fight back. Laurie wanted a girl. The plan was Laurie's but it was mine too. It would be good to see it cry and no Mam there to kiss it better. We did not say what we would do after we got the kid to our secret place. Laurie always had the ideas. And when I thought of the plan and the red diamond was hard in my belly, then I had some things I wanted to do for myself. Because everyone kicks me around but after this they would not kick me around any more.

We did not talk about that part. Laurie was right that if we said too much it would all come out and then we would get in big trouble for doing nothing and life would go on the same.

I said, I just saw a kid run off from his Dad but we don't stand a chance, they are all watching their kids.

~ No, that's no good. One kid is too easy to watch. What we want is a big family with lots of kids and a mother who is tired out and needs a rest. All it takes is five minutes. One of them wanders away a bit. We talk to it and take its hand and in a very short time we are lost in the crowd.

~ Suppose someone sees us go off with it?

~ Suppose they do? If they stop us we say it was lost and we were helping it find its Mummy. I'll do the talking. I have a nice voice. Grownups believe me.

The way he is telling it, I know it will happen for real. And soon because the fair is only on for a week. One week is all we have.

~ Okay. Tomorrow?

~ No, not tomorrow. Bank Holiday Monday. Millions of people will be here. We can even go on some things first.

~ Suppose your Dad comes with you?

~ He won't come, he hates fairs, they are too unhygienic.

I don't think anyone can actually stop it happening now. Micka can be in it or not. It won't make any difference. He won't dare tell anyone anything. But I feel that he wants to do it as much as I do and I think I have him sized up right in my mind. Anyway, who would do anything to stop it if he did tell? His family is just a bunch of sad losers. We will have this adventure, because the fair is just the perfect place and this is the perfect time. Every night I bite the bone for luck. It reminds me of Polly. Whatever we will do with our victim girl after the kidnap I think there will be biting in it.

So, the Day came. It was Bank Holiday Monday. I knew from when I first woke up and saw the sun it was a good day for the plan, just as I had said it would be. I got dressed and put the bone in my pocket.

Josie was still in bed. I went in to see her. She sort of woke up and wanted to know what I was doing. I told her, eating some cold sausages. She said she did not want to see me standing over her bed eating sausages or anything else. I said goodbye. She said, Goodbye, where are you going? I said, See you later. She lay back down in bed and pulled the cover over her head. So I didn't bother to tell her where I was going. Her handbag was on the chair in the kitchen. It was open a little bit. I could see her purse inside. If I had asked her she would have given me ten pounds. I took ten pounds and some change. Mothers should get up and look after their children in the mornings.

I was ready to go out by the front door when I saw the letter on the mat. It was addressed to Josie, in my father's handwriting. I picked it up. It was very light. There were two other letters for her. I put them on the hall table and looked at myself in the mirror and held the letter up to the mirror so I could see my father's writing back to front. I said to my reflection, I am going to count to fifty and if she doesn't come downstairs I will take this letter with me.

Because of the counting I wasn't concentrating like I normally do. I was listening with my ears on stalks to hear if she was moving about upstairs. I had to force myself not to count too quickly, to give her a chance to come down. So instead of thinking calmly about what we were going to do later, and what we might need, I was staring at myself and counting, and when I got to fifty I quickly shoved the letter in my jacket and opened the front door and ran down the path and out of sight of the house. You can see from this I am not a bad person, because stealing her letter made me feel so nervous. I honestly had never done anything like that before. The further away I got from her, the happier I became. My plan was to get into the fair and find a place to read the letter. It felt like having a present to open. I was going to read a secret message meant only for my parents' eyes. However much you think you know what they say to each other, it is really only guesswork.

The fair was open from ten o'clock in the morning and there were thousands of people there by the time I got in. The sun was shining and everyone was on holiday. I got caught up in the crowds and the excitement; every time I thought about the adventure my heart gave a little swoop. There were so many babies and little kids everywhere, and so many mothers looking tired, and the noise made it hard for them to concentrate on looking after their children carefully. I could feel that we were going to be lucky. Then I saw my target. There was a girl not much older than me and she was in charge of four children. She had a double kind of buggy with two of them in and the others were pulling at her and she kept looking over her shoulder. I had a thought that she was not supposed to be at the fair and I got as close as I could and tried to listen. Then she met a friend and they talked and I heard every word they said.

~ So, how long can you stay?

~ Mam will be back at five and she'll kill me—

~ What do we do with the bairns if we want to go on the gallopers?

~ We'll have to take it in turns. How much money have you got?

The children were all pulling and whining at her to go here and there and they went off to the baby roundabout. The two biggest children went on the baby roundabout and I had a few goes on the penny rollers and from there I could take a good look at the two little ones. One was a rather ugly boy with a fat face and a nappy. The other one was a little girl and she was quite pale and thin and every time I saw her she was quiet, which was good. The boy was bawling a lot, but she just looked around with her big eyes. And she had gingery coloured long hair and it was in ringlets but no ribbons. She had on a white and pink dress and black shiny shoes and white socks with lace bits on the top. I don't know how to tell how old kids are but I would guess maybe she was two or three. I liked it that she never made any noise. That was a good sign. I wondered, if I was to undo the strap of the buggy, would she get out on her own? Would she hold my hand like Shelley or would she eat some sweets if I gave them to her? I could hardly wait to get close to her when the big girls were chattering but I knew that I must be patient, like I was with the duck. Reading my father's letter would pass the time. I leaned up against the swing-boat stall and got it out of my pocket. I had a choice. I could tear it open, or try and open it like a spy and stick it back down again. I tried the spy method, but it started to tear even though I was being really careful. In the end I couldn't wait. I tore the envelope and read the letter.

My dear Josie,

I have done as you asked and made the appointment for Laurence. In my opinion you are over-reacting. I do not consider that he is in any way disturbed or difficult. He is quiet because he thinks a great deal. And I must say, Josie, that your own behaviour is verging on the eccentric, which makes me question whether you are the best judge of the boy's mental state. However, we shall know when Dr. Ramsay has seen him. He is an eminent child psychiatrist and I have enormous respect for his opinion.

As to the other matter, I leave it to you when and how you tell Laurence about my plans. It may not be of any interest to you, but this post at Adelaide University is a prestigious appointment for me and I cannot let a broken family stand in the way of the professional opportunity of a lifetime. I understand your irritation at the extra child care this move will involve. I am genuine in my offer to pay for Laurie to fly over to see me twice a year. I really do not know what else I can do. Your duties as a parent are not onerous and with our son away at school you will have the time to do whatever it is you need to do.

There is no need whatsoever to tell him that you have read his diary –

I felt as if I had been punched loads of times, worse than when Lee beat me up. It was actually hard to breathe. If I had been somewhere private I think I might even have cried. But I never got to finish reading the letter because the very next minute Micka was right there in front of me. I stuffed the letter in my pocket and we walked on together. I could stop this awful thinking for a while. It was such a relief to be doing something.

So I went back to the fair to do Laurie's plan. Lee came back to the flat from his slag last night; she threw him out. I was in bed and I heard him in the kitchen punching the walls and roaring. He was in a mood to kill. Mam was out shopping with Paula and Kevo was off doing the windscreen cleaning job so it was only Lee and me in the flat and I had to get out before he got up. There was not even school to get away to, it was holidays. So I went to Royts Lane. Laurie was there by the swingboats. I asked him was the plan on and he said yes and I wanted it as much as he did. He showed me the two big girls and the little kids in the twin buggy and we waited and the other kids got off the roundabout and the girls took them to buy ice cream.

The girls went on the chairoplane but they took turns. Then they wanted to go on the dodgems and they stood all the kids together round the buggy and bought them more lollies and candy floss and told them to keep still. The dodgems started and the small girl tried to get out the buggy and in the crowd Laurie bent over and let out the strap and the girl got out and stood by the buggy a minute and we waited would the others see and they were all screaming and shouting at the big girls in the car, bumping the boys and laughing. And we got nearer and nearer to this girl in a pink dress and her face was all dirty with the candy floss. And Laurie reaches down his hand and she holds her hand up to his hand and he is speaking real soft.

~ Shall we find your Mummy?

And we go on walking away and away from the fair and she lets us. I hold out my hand and she takes it and that is it. Me on the one side of her and Laurie on the other, holding her hands. And Laurie talks all the time and her hand is soft in mine. And she never cries or looks behind and no one comes running to stop us.

We had not thought where to go but the field is a big one and down one end is a hill and a stile and we get to the stile and she won't go over it. And then she starts crying for her Mam and Laurie puts his hand over her mouth and goes shush shush shush. Look at the daisies. She goes quiet and sits on the grass and Laurie takes the bone from his pocket and holds it over her head.

~ See, this is how I do it.

Then we hear people coming and we sit down real quick

with the girl. Two women and a man are walking to the stile and they climb over. Laurie says real cool, Going to the fair? It's great. We have to bring our sister home or we'd still be there.

~ She looks very tired.

Laurie nods his head so cool.

~ Yeah, that's why we're taking her home.

We get up off the grass and he picks her up.

~ Climb over and I'll give her to you.

She is heavier than Paula and she smells of candy floss. I put her down and we are over the stile. There is a track which goes to the canal but there will be people there today. The other way goes down a hill. So we walk on down that way and Laurie thinks what to do.

~ We have to find a place that no one uses, a safe place, Laurie says. Let's go on down the hill. So we go on down and there is a wood and a gate. We get over the gate and we try and lift her over but Laurie drops her and she has a bang on her arm and he covers up her mouth with his hand.

~ Stop crying or I'll smack you. He takes his hand away and she opens her mouth and roars and he smacks her face. Then she shuts up.

~ Is this it? Is this the safe place?

~ I don't know. I've done fucking everything so far. You do something for a change.

~ Her arm looks funny.

~ So?

~ It looks bad.

~ Well, I've had a broken arm and it doesn't hurt that much. Are you saying we should stop the plan because of a stupid broken arm?

Laurie pushes me and I fall in the bramble bush and he stands over the girl and he gives her a kick, but a small one only.

~ This is what we're here for. This was the plan.

He pushes her again with his foot and she falls and she cries with her mouth in the earth.

~ Your Mammy can't hear. You're ours now.

But she cries on and on.

~ You be a good girl and don't cry. If you don't cry we won't hurt you. Maybe we'll take you home after.

Laurie pulls me up and says in my ear real soft, After what? What are we here for?

~ Kidnap.

~ And? Kidnap and?

~ Kidnap and . . . do things like you said.

She lifted up her face from the earth. Her dress was up and I could see her little belly. Laurie had some chocolate buttons. He gave her some and she took them and stopped the noise. It was good when she did not cry. Her bad arm was hanging down funny. Then the buttons was finished. She was rubbing at her eye with her hand but there was dirt on her hand and she looked like she was going to cry some

198

more. I tried to go away in my head, but it was all fixed, I was pinned like in the dream—

~ It was your plan too, Micka. Get a stray girl, get her into our power, and do what we like with her. Remember?

I shoved my hand over his mouth. He was so sure. He made me feel like a babby myself. I did not want to hear about the fucken plan. Not now, when I was so cold in my guts and she was real, really holding our hand and we could see her face.

~ You think you're so smart. Kill Lee, you said, kill him with the bone. You and your fucken bone—

Laurie's hand was in his pocket. He brought it out. The bone was in his hand and it was pointing at me.

~ Want to know the last time I used this?

~ When? When did you use it? On Lee? What fucken use was that?

~ Want to know who I used it on? Your gyppo friend.

Then I did know from his face. He did it. He did it to Blue.

~ Blue was cut, the cut went bad, his Nan told me.

~ *After* I pointed the bone. Like I'm doing to you now, but I said the words. Here and here and here. I did it the day after the Earth Tribe wankers came. You know I didn't go back there any more after that. Now you know why.

~ You can't prove it was you.

~ I can actually, snotface. It's in the letter. I bet you haven't dared open it.

~ Kill Lee, I said. Kill Lee. He's still here. You cannat do it. You cannat do anything but talk.

~ Shut up! Shut up! You're ruining everything!

We were in the woods now. I thought he would start the plan then. But he left. Left me and the stray girl. Ran away down into the woods and the dark was coming. The red diamond was there now, stronger than ever, and if there was a plan there was only me to do it.

How could I be so stupid? Wasting time on arguments when we had the girl and it was only a matter of time before someone came looking for her. What an idiot I was to start boasting about killing Blue. What were we here to do? I tried to be like a scientist and think about experiments and the ideas I had about biting, but I was on a roundabout of thoughts that went up and down like the gallopers at the fair, faster and faster, till I felt sick. Thanks to that filthy letter of my father's I had brought no weapons, unless you count the bone. But the bone, if it worked, never worked fast. We could not wait until the next day. The plan was that we both went home before our families suspected anything. I think we had discussed that. But now I felt that I never wanted to see Josie again, ever. Plotting to get me put away as a lunatic! She had read my log book. She had invaded my bedroom, she had read all my secret thoughts, and I expect she had a good laugh at how pathetic I was as she planned her revenge.

It was so hard to concentrate. We had thought about this plan for months, but we never said exactly how we were going to show our power when the moment came. And we were here now, it was all ready; but I felt no power at all. I had run away. And whatever I was running from was chasing me like a bear in the woods. Why couldn't I stop this awful thinking? Just escape, get away from everything? But if I did that, wouldn't I be weak and a doormat for ever?

I was in the deepest part of the wood now. I saw something gleaming in the dark. A long piece of rope made of some twisted yellow stuff. Strong as wire. Perfect. You could say it was a sign from fate. Or luck. Rope could be used as a weapon – or we could tie the girl up and then decide what to do next.

I had to make myself keep moving, go back to the girl and Micka, because there were too many questions now in my head, quiet at first, then shouting, sounding like my mother, or Mr. Overson. I had to shut them up. I had to show some power. In the wood it was almost too dark to see. I had to get into Phase Four at last.

But when I got back, things were different. Things happened. Things we had not planned.

*

How did Lee know to find us? How did he know to jump out at me with no sound? He was smiling.

~ *What's going on here? A party, is it? Can anyone join in?*

I felt his breath close on my neck. Smell of whiskey. His hand on his wolf belt, ready. I let go of the bairn. I couldn't move. Like in my dream, pinned.

~ *Here's your little friend come back, calls himself the Devil. Well, Devil Boy, let's see what you can do.*

Laurie should have run. He should have fucked off when he had the chance. He stood staring, and for once he had no words. It was like Lee had a string and he pulled the string and we came along, like dogs.

~ *You two are up to something with this bairn. Go ahead. Don't mind me.*

Laurie was holding a long rope but he dropped the rope.

~ *See, that's your trouble. Bullshitters. Gobshites.*

Lee went down on his knees by the girl. Softly, making no sound. Saw her crooked arm. Stood up. Pointed at us.

~ *I'd say you broke it. Bad boys.*

Lee is pulling us, pulling us closer. The girl sitting like she is tired, with her mouth open. Too tired to cry even, or get away. Lee is walking on the leaves, soft like a cat, and his eyes – we have to look at his eyes.

~ *So what are yiz up to? Little fucking Professor here and his tame monkey?*

~ Fuck off. Fuck you.

My voice soft like a girl's. Talking to a deaf man. Lee laughing. Stands at the back of me. His eyes drilling into my head. The rope. Lying on the black earth like a snake. Fucken yellow rope. Lee's colour. Why did Laurie bring that yellow rope? My worst colour. My very worst.

~ *Watch your partner in crime, Mr. Bigmouth. See how quiet he is. Want to see what he has? The knife that Mikey cut throats with? That blade, that's real. Time for action, bonny lads.*

My eyes went shut. Was it Lee put the rope in my hand? I did not see the other end, where it went. Only his voice in my ear, always his fucken voice.

Only one way now. Down. After you come out of this wood, things will never be the same again.

CHAPTER 10

Afterwards

Dark now. So dark in the wood. I could hear the small little twigs breaking under my foot.

How had they gone so still? Under my hand I feel a face. Wet. Rope round neck, wet.

Then I am away from there, running on a path. In my head, a picture. Blue and me, the way to the canal. Sunny that day. Nice. Him and me. The broken wall, the water. Washing, careful. Not to cut the finger. Go like Blue, dead in the ambulance, blood and mud mixing. Lamplight by the canal showed my hand yellow. Wearing the red sweater like in my dream. Red never shows blood. Throw it in anyway. Uncle Mikey's knife slid under the water like a silver pike fish with teeth shining. In my dream the talking fish had eyes like a baby. Don't, it said, don't, Micka.

Uncle Mikey's knife. One thing Laurie did not know.

Lee was laughing all through. Lee liked it. He did not say

stop. But what came out of me, that was from Lee. I swear it was.

Home. Only Mam and Paula. Paula was having a bath in the sink. No Lee.

~ Michael, where have you been all day?

~ I was at the fair.

~ Look at the state of you. All over mud. Will you wash your face and give her a bottle while I have a smoke, son?

I gave Paula her bottle. It was warm milk, with sugar in, and she sucked with her eyes wide open looking up at me so soft and floppy and baby pink. I smelled her head and it was sweet as the sugar milk and I breathed in her baby smell and her baby world and all I wanted was to go to sleep and not to dream at all.

~ Ah, look how she loves her big brother, Mam said. We sat like that for a while and Paula went to sleep in my arms and Mam kissed me and sang a song to the baby.

All on a sudden I was tired and I went to bed. Under my bed was my school bag and I remembered what was in it. The letter that Laurie gave me. The letter he said proved everything.

I opened it. There was a drawing Laurie done of the bone. Not a good drawing. Lee, and a snake, with a cross by them both. And a gypsy trailer and the end of the bone pointing at the window of the trailer. Inside a boy lying on the bed. Blue. Another cross over his head.

I turned the page. Two boys. One with red hair. Holding their arms together. Blood dripping. Words: *We both did it all. Blood Brothers.*

The letter was like someone there in the room pulling my hair and twisting the skin on my wrist. Blue was a good man. Who showed Laurie the way to Royts Lane? Who let Laurie at him? Laurie and his fucken bone. It was him killed the snake, not me. He was only supposed to kill Lee.

I went to tear up the note, but on the ceiling where the tiger was springing down at me was a new mark. Just an eye. Leave it, said the eye. I left it.

I was asleep, then they came. Police. I heard Mam go to the door. I stood by the window, ready to jump like Kevo. Down, Lee said, from now on it is only down. I was not ready for them. I had no thoughts properly to say what it was we did in the wood. I would run in the dark till they caught me.

Then a cry from Mam. Calling me.

I went back in the kitchen. Two police, one a woman, Mam sitting and the woman holding her hand like she was sorry.

~ O my God, O my sweet Jesus God, Mam was singing like a prayer. She pulled me to her. The police let her. One tries to smile at me but her eyes stay cold, watching me, waiting.

~ O, Michael, the worst, the very worst.

~ No, Mam, nothing—

206

~ It's your brother— The man put his face down next to mine. He had blue bristles on his whole face nearly.

~ What brother?

~ It's Lee, Lee, God love him. He's dead! Mam is rocking like a baby.

~ I never touched him.

The police shakes his head.

~ No, bonny lad, he was in the Badger. A fight.

~ In the pub? He's dead? He died in the pub?

~ There was witnesses, Mam is crying, he got himself into a fight, it was three onto one—

The police is looking at me. I can't see right, I fall. Someone picks me up.

~ Oh, he is in shock—

I need to know when, when he was in the fight, but I cannot ask. Mam is crying. She has to go to see Lee to identify the body.

The body.

~ We'll come back in the morning, Mrs. Doyle, says the woman police, have you anyone can come in and sit with you?

~ I have Michael, says Mam. She is pinching my arm but I make no noise. He's a good boy and he will mind me, won't you, son?

The police is gone.

*

Then it was morning and the rain lashing at the windows and the wind screaming.

Mam did not sleep all night. She was waiting for the police to come and bring her to the hospital to see the body.

But when they came, there were four of them.

~ Mrs. Doyle, has your son said anything about what he was doing yesterday?

~ Mrs. Doyle, can we see the clothes he came home in?

~ Mrs. Doyle, have you ever heard him mention a friend called Laurie Parker?

~ Did you see the news this morning?

~ Did Michael know a little girl called Tracy Gerrard?

Mam said, It was on the early news. She was at the fair.

~ She was abducted from the fair, Mrs. Doyle, taken to Walkenstown Woods by the canal.

The police have their books ready to write in.

~ Michael, were you at the fair yesterday?

~ That poor bairn, Mam says, her mother must be frantic—

~ She was found wandering in the woods last night with a broken arm—

~ It was not me broke her arm. It was Laurie, it was all Laurie—

~ Laurie Parker's body was found this morning. What do you know about this, Michael?

~ Tell us the truth, Michael. It will all come out in the end.

I tell the truth. They don't believe me.

CHAPTER 11
November 1999

Every day I wake up. The walls here are yellow. I could put up pictures, if I wanted. My curtains are dark blue, like canal water.

They still ask me do I want to do any Art in the workshop. Art therapy, it is called. Everything here is called therapy. There is a garden and carpentry. They have given me lessons to learn to write and speak better. But words take other things away. Colours and shapes I used to dream with have gone for ever.

Night comes and I go to bed. I take the pills to help with the nightmares. In the morning I wake up. The walls are still yellow.

Outside, more people have died. Uncle Mikey and Gran, and Kevo died in a car crash. Paula is okay, but she doesn't live with our Mam any more. She has a foster home. They bring her to visit me one time on her birthday. She has a pink dress and her hair is clean and done up with ribbons. She talks posher than me.

Mam does not come.

But all the talk here is life, Micka, your future, don't live in the past. Dead people are not your future. Say you are sorry for what you did and move on.

I think I am on the same pills my Mam used to take.

Yesterday I had a meeting with my key worker who is called Deirdre. She says she likes art and paintings. Says she can bring me prints of pictures from a museum to put on my walls. All I have to do is choose. But when she talks I get a heavy feeling in my belly. That is her world, museums and pictures and theatres, like Miss Glennie used to tell me. That world is not for me.

Deirdre is trying to get me to draw. Every time she comes to see me she brings some different art stuff. Pencils, charcoals, water colours. Today she has some kind of painting chalks. She pushes them over to me. She shows how if you wet your finger and smudge the chalk, it goes like oil painting, like magic. Pastel crayons, she calls them.

~ Just play with them. You don't even have to try and draw anything, she says. But a bit later she starts again.

~ I know you are good at drawing and you used to love it. Why not just give it a go?

Because that was the old life. Much good it did me.

~ You will be coming up for review soon, Michael. Before you leave here and go to the Young Offenders' Unit, they will ask if you have made progress. I would love to be able to show them.

She thinks a picture is progress. Let her try to see some good in this one.

I take the magic pastel crayons and close my eyes and it comes on the page straight away. It is the picture I always see, when I let it come.

A yellow river with a few red worms wriggling along the bank.

In the water, drowning, with mouth open and crying for help, he is dying.

Blue is standing on the bank, fishing. He does not see the boy drowning.

That boy is the fish. And like eels wriggling, the two of them are coming at him with their saw-edge teeth. Slowly he is drowning and the black water worms are waiting for him. Waiting to swim out and begin the long slow business of eating his face.

The picture says it, and I feel it in my gut. I am the fish that talked.

I never want to see their faces again but they are in my dreams, pills or no pills.

The doctors say there is no point in blaming the dead.

~ Who is this one? asks Deirdre, like she doesn't know.

~ Lee.

~ Now, Michael, she says so soft and kind, you know right well that Lee is not to blame for what happened. We have proved it to you. The injuries to Laurence, your finger prints

... the witnesses in the pub. Lee could not have been there.

Then what would I draw him for? They say he died in a fight at the Badger the exact same time as he was in the woods laughing and driving me mad. But he was there. I swear it would not have happened without him there. And did I bring the knife, or did he? Maybe without Lee, no one would have died.

~ And who's this one? she asks, and she is kind, like always.

~ It's him.

Always there, always in my head. He started it. All this is his fault.

Laurie. An eel. Twisting and wriggling for ever in my dreams.

May he rot in hell.

Deirdre makes a sigh and puts the crayons away.

~ Can I not keep them, Miss?

Deirdre is not smiling now. She puts on her coat.

~ Oh, Michael. What am I going to do with you?

~ Leave the crayons, Miss.

~ I've three other boys to see today. You're not the only one who likes to draw, you know.

She sits down again, fiddling with the pale blue scarf round her neck.

~ One of them is getting out next week. A boy your age. He's done his time, like you. He's sorry for what he did. That's

212

why you're here. To let go of being angry. With them and with yourself.

~ Did he kill? Is he as bad as me?

I don't care if he did or not. I don't want to know. I say this to make her go. I want her to fuck off.

~ Oh, Michael.

Deirdre's mouth is in a straight line now and she gets up and picks up her bag.

~ I'll see you next week. And the next. And the next. Just try, Michael. Please.

She is gone.

And the next. And the next. And the next.

EPILOGUE: 2004

Another world

April. Grey rain spits on the window.

I am shaving. Some boys learn this from their fathers. Some by watching big brothers. Or uncles. A prison barber taught me the day before they let me out. He only had twenty minutes. But with me, I see a thing once, and I never forget it. The picture is in my head for ever.

I hear the post van. Go downstairs and there's a letter on the mat. The Social Services mark on the envelope, and an English stamp. The only people in the world now who know where I am and who I was.

I make some tea and roll a fag. Yes, this is a kind of freedom. I am a legal person here. I don't need the pills any more. I don't have nightmares. It cost me. But in the end, the dead and I have made a sort of truce.

No one tells me what to do. I can go out or stay in bed and not give a fuck about anyone and they don't have to give a fuck about me.

I open the letter.

To my dear brother,

Thank you for the picture 'My House' that you sent for my birthday. I had a great time. We had a Barbie party and everyone brought their Barbies and we dressed them up and had a picnic in the garden. And I had ten candles on my cake to blow out, and I did it first time with no help.

I was nine. I had a cake. We were in the hostel. Fourteen other screaming kids to share it with.

My Auntie Carol is helping me to write this on the computer so it will be spelled right. She says I could call her Mam now and Uncle Derek could be Dad because they have adopted me for ever and maybe I will call them that soon because at school the other girls have Mams and now I do too. But I always called them Auntie and Uncle because of the fostering before.

A mam and a dad. What everyone should have. Not given by signing papers. Born with.

Your picture is beautiful. I like the little windows on the house and the green roof and the dog asleep on the front step. I hope it is your real house. I know you are in a country far away and even you have a different name and we don't know what it is, so Auntie Carol says I can choose a name to call you. I think Steve is a good name for a big brother. Do you like that name?

Dream on, little sister. You can't know anything about me for sure. I am a drawing that is half done. You will have to fill in the colours for yourself.

I remember when we came to see you in the Home when I was five. I knew straight away you were my brother because our hair is the same colour and you were looking sad but when I showed you the picture of Mrs. Simpkins, my hamster, you smiled and then you looked kind.

Well that hamster is still alive but she is really really old now. She is very gentle and she never bites, not even when the kitten got on top of her cage.

I hope the dog in the picture is a real dog and your friend.

Yes. The dog is real. A stray no one else wanted. He bites, but only when I go away too long and leave him on his own.

I will try and draw me as a ballerina because I love ballet but my drawing is rubbish so please do not laugh at my picture.

Why would I laugh? I see you now, little skinny legs in rose-pink tights and a sticking-out skirt. Smiling, freckles, red hair up in a ponytail. Kid sister. My kid sister.

The dog licks my hand. It is wet, salt.

Uncle Derek, I mean my Dad, has made a frame and put up your picture on our kitchen wall.

It is good I have you for my brother and I hope one day we will meet again.

Your loving sister,

Paula

Paula's world. My painting, a safe part of me, on her wall. A mam and a dad. And a far away big brother. She calls him Steve.

When I see her name, I see the baby with Kevo giving her the bottle drinking beer and her nappy not changed and her face all red and twisted up with crying.

How would we meet? Where? What can I say to her?

I see Deirdre's face and hear her soft voice: She's just a kid. She deserves a chance. Be happy for her.

Watching other people be happy does not bring me good feelings. I think I hate her. And her kind Mam and Dad and her gentle guinea pig and all the stuff that was there for other kids that I never even knew about. A right to be minded.

Parties and presents. Too late now. Even the dog that's mine bites me. That's what I get.

I break things. I kill things. I am bad luck.

The best I can do for Paula is never to come into her world.